Books by Philip Loraine

And to My Beloved Husband

The Break in the Circle

The Angel of Death

Day of the Arrow

W. I. L. One to Curtis

The Dead Men of Sestos

A Mafia Kiss

Photographs Have Been Sent to Your Wife

Voices in an Empty Room

VOICES IN AN EMPTY ROOM

VOICES IN AN EMPTY ROOM

Philip Loraine

RANDOM HOUSE
NEW YORK

Library of Congress Cataloging in Publication Data

Loraine, Philip, pseud.
    Voices in an empty room.

    I. Title.
PZ3.L8838Vo3   [PR6062.067]   823'.9'14   73–20598
ISBN 0–394–48949–7

Manufactured in the United States of America
First American Edition

9 8 7 6 5 4 3 2

Part I

THE
LIVING

One

THE WOMAN who sat at the table, her big hands resting on it, appeared to be holding a red-hot ember, and her expression, which seemed to be one of extreme pain, did nothing to dispel the illusion. In fact, if the sagging London November afternoon could have summoned up enough light, it would have revealed that what she was holding was an egg—an Easter egg, clearly by Fabergé: crimson enamel resplendent with rubies and pink pearls, pinpointed with diamonds, a magnificent piece.

Suddenly, violently, she pushed the thing away from her so that it spun on the worn polish of the table, flashing fire. She rubbed her hands together as if they had indeed been burned, staring at the jeweled object with distaste, even fear. "No," she said, "I can have nothing to do with this. Nothing!"

A smaller, elegant woman who sat opposite her leaned forward, watching the revolving egg until it whispered to a standstill. "Why not?"

"It . . . would be dangerous."

The other picked it up and looked at it thoughtfully. "Why do you think it's dangerous?"

"In my profession one senses these things. Is it stolen?"

"*I* certainly didn't steal it."

"I'm sorry, I didn't mean . . ."

"It may well have been stolen at some point in its career. People do steal beautiful and valuable things."

The big, shabby woman continued to stare, frowning. "There is . . . blood on it. I cannot handle it."

The other woman turned her eyes from the jeweled magnificence and looked at the defeated face confronting her, at the worn clothes; then at the worn room slipping towards evening loneliness and the inadequate meal prepared on the cooker hidden behind a curtain in the corner; then at the dank November trees and the red Edwardian ugliness of Earl's Court outside the window. Finally: "I think perhaps you will do as I ask, if only because I'm a very rich woman."

"Money has nothing to do with it."

On the battered sideboard there reposed a hideous yellow bowl holding two unripe bananas and a shriveled orange. Her eyes on this, and pulling her mink coat a little closer about her, for the room was also cold, the rich and elegant woman said, "Money has something to do with everything." There was an edge of sadness in her tone.

TWO

JOHN LAMB'S instincts were as deeply buried as those of any other so-called civilized man. Only in retrospect—which is to say, too late—could he recognize the danger signals he had managed to ignore so successfully at the time. There had been no answer when he had called San Francisco from New York: well, he hadn't given her much warning of his approach, because he himself had not known until the last moment exactly when he would be able to leave Paris; and since she had been away from home for nearly a year, there would be a hundred people she'd want to see and who would want to see her. In any case, as he well knew, she soon grew bored with her own company; she liked to be out and about. Then there was his reply-paid telegram, which had evinced no reply: not really surprising, when he had sent it so late; he doubted whether she would even be at the airport to meet him.

The plane, banking in a cloudless sky, catching the last of the setting sun, revealed a West Coast already touched by night, revealed also a soft wall of fog moving in from the Pacific; even as he caught his first glimpse of the Golden Gate, fog obscured it. Instinct reacted to this as best it might, but he subdued the quick turn in the stomach, telling himself that it was ridiculous. In addition, he told himself again that if he had really expected her to meet him at the airport, he should have sent that telegram at least a day earlier. He told himself that the slow-burning uneasiness which had begun to smolder inside him was the direct result of Time, nothing else. After all, he had spent a mere two days in New York, so that now, at five-thirty on a foggy San Franciscan evening, it was in fact two A.M. by Paris (and his body's) reckoning; he was tired, that was all.

"The man who listens to Reason," as Bernard Shaw roundly pronounced, "is lost." It is presumably only a matter of how long it takes him to realize it.

In order to dispel any unreasonable thoughts, Lamb engaged the taxi-driver in breezy conversation, learning that San Francisco was the most beautiful city in the world, that the fog had arrived early, not being expected until the small hours of the morning, that otherwise it was the finest January for many years, that over three hundred people had committed suicide by jumping off the Golden Gate Bridge since its opening, that the taxi-driver's wife had made an idiot of herself at Magnin's sale, that the part of the city for which he was bound was an extremely classy one, inhabited only by the very rich, and that if he wanted a woman the taxi-driver knew where to take him.

By the time they reached Number 337 Gilman Street, the fog—a blowing melodramatic fog such as he had never seen before—had obliterated the city.

The woman who eventually opened the door was large and shapeless, with wispy grey hair which she kept pushing back from her round face with fingers like uncooked chippolata sausages; she was dressed in vague brown wool. Behind him the sound of the departing taxi dwindled abruptly, giving the impression that it had passed through a door somewhere out there in the fog, a door which had closed softly behind it, leaving him alone with this formless female. She now passed the sausages across washed-out greenish eyes and said, "Not here. No one of this name." She had vestiges of a French accent. He saw himself lost in a strange city, in the wrong city, for all he knew; he had no proof, beyond the vanished taxi-driver, that this was indeed San Francisco. Lost, enveloped in endless fog, wandering from steep street to steep street with two heavy suitcases, looking for a house that didn't exist and a girl who didn't exist.

From within the house, a sharp incisive voice said, with a kind of weary impatience, "Oh Lulu, you know the name perfectly well. In the stable."

He was so staggered by the unlikelihood of this immense knitted tea cozy being called Lulu that he had no time to analyze the odd variety of expressions which managed to cross her face before she said, "Of course, what is the matter with me? Miss Eleanor!"

"That's right."

"In the stable." She gestured out into the fog and vaguely to the left of the house. He caught a nuance of unwashed armpit as she lowered her arm again. Then she withdrew, swiftly for one so large, and closed the massive door in his face.

He went down the grandiose steps of what he had imagined to be Ellie's house, turned and stared up at its façade. It seemed to him even more fantastic than it had at first glance (but then, he did not as yet know anything about the architectural caprices of which

Pacific Heights was capable), a colossal jumble of ill-assorted styles, made more unreal by the shifting fog-light of the streetlamps; it had apparently sprouted some kind of pinnacled turret since he had first looked at it. At the back of his mind was an impression of Ellie, outcast, seen through the legs of horses, huddled in the straw at a corner of the stables, exercising her well-known propensity for doing nothing about any situation which had become too much for her.

He walked to the left of the house and discerned an elegantly pedimented archway through which a narrow cobbled lane pitched sharply downhill towards a dim glow of light. He put down his suitcases and went to investigate. The cobbled lane ran along the side of the house for what seemed a long way and then opened out into what was evidently a cobbled yard. The stables had naturally been turned into garages, and after some searching, he came upon a white-painted wooden staircase leading to an upper floor and two cozily lighted windows. He climbed the stairs and discovered a white door with a brass knocker in the shape of a seahorse. Under the knocker was lodged a piece of damp paper on which was written large in Ellie's unmistakable and childish hand, "Back about 5." If he could have felt that the note was addressed solely to him, it might have been some consolation, but he couldn't convince himself of it. His telegram was probably reposing somewhere inside that vast pinna-cled house which towered above him, and to which he had addressed it, ignored by that vast French-origined nitwit who had opened the door to him. He banged the knocker, not hopefully, and waited a full minute listen-ing to silence broken only by the sound of some ship bellowing like a wounded mastodon down in the Bay. Then he sighed, replaced the soggy note, and went back down the staircase. It was now ten minutes to seven o'clock.

He paused, stood for a time in the cobbled yard, uncertain, looking at the back of the big house in which no light showed; then he remembered his suitcases, abandoned on the sidewalk, or possibly already spirited away into the fog by some passer-by.

He had not particularly noticed the car parked in front of the house, largely because there were cars parked at intervals along what he could see of the street. As he bent to pick up the suitcases, however, he was surprised to notice that somebody was sitting inside it, watching him; watching, he supposed, everything he had done since his arrival. He found this for some reason unnerving. He stared at the car and at its half-seen occupant, wondering if it had anything to do with Ellie, and if it had, just how he could broach the subject. While he was staring, a male voice said, "You're John, I guess."

"Yes." Hopefully, he went nearer, and found himself looking at what he initially took to be a boy of perhaps eighteen: a good-looking, somewhat elfin face; very bright blue eyes regarding him from under a dashing fur hat à la Russe, on which the fog sat in beads.

"John Lamb," the boy said. "It's a divine name." He batted his eyelashes a little and smiled. He added, at the exact moment that it struck John Lamb how like Ellie he was, "I'm Ellie's brother—I'm Richard."

It was typical of Ellie that she had never, in the five months they had lived together in Europe, mentioned that she possessed a brother. Uneasiness stirred again.

How strange it was—since he had clearly meant to make himself known in the end—that this odd young man had sat here for so long, hidden in his car, watching a stranger's very evident bewilderment and saying nothing.

"You wouldn't happen to know where she is."

Richard laughed. He had a remarkably deep laugh, a remarkably deep voice altogether, considering the elfin look and the coquettish manipulation of the eyelashes. " 'You wouldn't happen to know where she is.' I adore that, it's so British. I was in London last summer." He had stopped laughing, and now, with narrowed eyes and lips compressed, no longer looked eighteen, but nearer twenty-five, which was his actual age. He said, "I've no idea *where* she is, but I've a darn good idea what she's doing. Your girlfriend, Mr. Lamb, is screwing my boyfriend—how does that grab you?"

John Lamb was twenty-seven, which he considered to be a pretty ripe age. Though he lived in France, and vastly preferred it to his native country, this didn't stop him being a thoroughly British Briton; he possessed a very unruly temper, it's true, but it was not roused easily; he also believed in reason; he had a suspicion that certain kinds of Americans were given to making unnecessarily dramatic, and indeed, rather common, remarks in order to draw attention to themselves; he had noticed that this habit was often shared by homosexuals, and could therefore be expected to occur with greater frequency in homosexuals who were also American. He said, "The least you could do is ask me to get into your car and out of this bloody fog. As far as I'm concerned, it's now four o'clock in the morning, and I never was any good at staying up all night."

When they were sitting side by side, Ellie's brother removed his Russian fur hat, revealing stylishly groomed fair hair, and said, "Why don't you tell me I'm a boring foul-mouthed faggot—that's what you're thinking."

"In the first place, that's not what I'm thinking; and in the second, I haven't known you long enough to be able to say whether that's what you are or not."

"Among other things, that's what I am." He sighed. "Life would be a whole lot easier if I didn't always get stuck with AC/DC's."

Lamb gave him an uncomprehending look, which made him laugh again. Laughing, he looked very like Ellie, so that Lamb's stomach turned over. Laughing, he said, "Oh come *on*, everybody in London knows what AC/DC means."

"I happen to live in Paris."

"Bisexual."

"Oh."

After a pause, and with a glance: "I suppose you aren't?"

"Actually, no."

Another sigh. "Stefan is. And though I shouldn't have said it, I really do think he and Ellie are screwing —you know what she's like."

John Lamb pondered this one for some time in silence. He had certainly imagined that he knew what Ellie was like, but did he? Did he in fact know anything about her at all; she had never even told him that she had this rococo brother. She had given him the address of a large house in which she didn't live. She had left a note saying that she would be back about five, and it was now seven-fifteen. Gloomily, he decided that the answer was, probably, No, he had no idea what Ellie was like. Ellie's brother reinforced this by adding, "Well, don't look so surprised, for Christ's sake—she shacked up with *you* for quite a while, didn't she?"

Lamb was on the point of saying, "That's a different matter altogether," when he realized how stupid, pompous, and unreasonable it would sound. Then he thought, Oh, to hell with how it sounds, and said it anyway: "That's a different matter altogether, I want her to marry me."

Richard looked at him for a while in silence; then said, "Oh Jesus, I'm sorry. Look, I can explain . . ."

"You don't have to."

"Yes, I do. I'd *never* have said that about screwing if I'd known you wanted to *marry* her. What's the matter with the dumb broad anyway, why didn't she tell me? Or doesn't she know?"

"She knows all right."

Ellie's brother, looking exactly like Ellie when she had committed some unalterable faux pas, gazed at him round-eyed and, he could have sworn, not far from tears. "Jesus!" he said angrily. "Why am I such a *prick?*"

"I assure you, it doesn't matter."

"Oh God! Don't start being British about it!"

"I'm afraid that's unavoidable."

"You know what I mean. And please listen, I really must explain—I'm a terribly jealous person by nature . . ."

"Then you should keep away from bisexuals, it would halve the field."

"You're so right. But what I mean is, I'm probably imagining this whole thing, and with Stefan being

Yugoslav—you know what *they're* like—and so goddam beautiful . . ."

Swiftly, materializing out of fog, another car slid to a
stop beside them, and John Lamb found himself
looking into Ellie's eyes. There was certainly no mistaking the look of total joy which illuminated her whole
face at the sight of him. He wound down his window
(hers was open anyway) and they kissed enthusiasti-
cally, faces cold with fog. There was also, Lamb
thought as they kissed, no mistaking the goddam
beauty of the young man who was sitting next to her,
watching the embrace with obvious astonishment.

Ellie said, "Oh darling! Oh Johnny, am I pleased to
see *you!*"

Richard leaned forward and looked beyond this
embrace at his friend. "For Christ's sake, get out of
that car, you dumb Slav—I've been waiting here more
than an hour!"

Ellie also turned and looked at Stefan, laughing:
"This is the man I'm going to marry."

Her brother laughed also. Stefan, who evidently
didn't find any of it at all funny, transferred himself
with alacrity from Ellie's car to Richard's; as he got
into it, Richard said, "If that goulash is ruined when we
get home, I'm going to let you have it right in the
kisser."

"Goulash," his friend replied, revealing strong peas-
ant practicality, "cannot ruin by overcook; improves
only."

"Where the hell have you been anyway?"

"Circus. You not wanting to go, Ellie take me, I am
most grateful."

"Right," said Ellie. "Surprised?" Her brother gave

her a long look; then transferred that vivid blue stare to John Lamb. They sorted themselves out, pair by pair, and parted. The gap in the curtains of Number 337, through which interested eyes had observed all this, was discreetly closed.

Ellie's cuckoo clock cuckooed nine times, loudly. Lamb, lying at rest in her soft arms, his cheek against her soft small breasts, smelling the charming and individual scent of her, knew with postsexual prescience that the cuckoo was all very well for lovers, but must not be allowed to follow them into marriage. Nine o'clock in San Francisco was six A.M. in Paris. His night was nearly over, which must be why, though he had not slept, he no longer felt sleepy; it was nearly time to wake up.

"All right," he said, "now explain about the house and fat French Lulu who opened the door to me. What's she doing in there anyway, running a bordello?"

Ellie giggled and sat up. She was the only girl he had ever known who handled nakedness with a perfect natural grace (artful grace was something else). Naked, she was a child. Her honey-colored hair, which she declined to wear fashionably long, had sprung back from fog-wetness into soft curls. He put a hand up to it and ran his fingers through it. Ellie purred. He said, "It really is natural."

"I told you it was."

"I didn't believe you."

"I don't tell lies."

It was on the tip of his tongue to say, "Then *did* you have sex with the Yugoslav?" but he controlled the desire, not wanting to spoil things. (Also, she happened to like circuses.)

"Lulu," said Ellie, "is the companion. It's rented to a Mrs. Guardi, Mrs. Amelia Guardi. Actually, I could have kicked Richie in the balls, he had no *right* to rent it, not without asking me first. Money, money, money, it's all he ever thinks about. And men, men, men."

"You were in Europe."

"Well, he could call me, for Christ's sake! He thinks nothing of calling his boring German boyfriend in Munich. It's not his house, it's *ours*. I'm hungry, how about you?"

"They did nothing but feed me on that plane."

"I'm going to have eggs and bacon—and mushrooms." She walked, naked, across the studio and into the kitchen.

Lamb lay in bed for a moment longer, looking at the big room and liking it. Then he roused himself and went after her. She was putting bacon into a pan. He said, "The fat will splutter and burn your tummy." Ellie took an apron from its hook and put it on.

"That's sexy," he said. "Even a bit kinky." The kitchen, like the studio, like Ellie herself, was immaculate. She liked clean bright colors and clean textures—scrubbed wood and tile. Everything about the place was eminently touchable, as she was herself. Touching and holding Ellie was a pleasure in its own right—not merely sexual. He said, "You never even told me that you owned the house. I thought it belonged to your father."

"It did. It was left to him by Uncle Hugh. Oh my God, our *family*! You have no idea! One day when it's raining and we're in bed—you know, afterwards—I'll tell you about them, they're wild, really wild. Uncle Phew! That's what Richie and I used to call him when we were little—he always looked as though he was smelling something nasty. Maybe he was, as far as we were concerned; the Owen Spensers and the Harold Spensers haven't been on speaking terms since about 1900. Uncle Phew was a Harold Spenser, Father's an Owen Spenser. Anyway"—she jumped back hastily as a mushroom spat at her—"after Hugh there weren't any more male Harold Spensers—he was a bachelor, whatever that means—so rather than let it go to just anybody, he left it to Father. Even an Owen Spenser is better than no Spenser at all." She grinned at him. "All this hoity-toity family crap must make you laugh—being English, I mean."

"Not at all, I think it's very upper. My grandfather was a plumber. God knows who his grandfather was!"

"We're supposed to go back to Edmund Spenser, the poet, but I say, if we do, how come they were all a bunch of crooks and not a bunch of poets? I say, the nearest we ever got to Edmund Spenser is the family motto."

"Which is?"

Ellie struck a pose, looking, in the bib-fronted apron and nothing else, like a stripper playing a cook in some burlesque finale. " 'And as she looked about, she did behold how over that same door was likewise writ, Be bold, be bold, and everywhere be bold.' " She returned to the mushrooms, which were burning.

"It's rather a long motto."

"We just have the last bit, 'Everywhere Be Bold.' It's written up over the front door, but you wouldn't have been able to see it for fog. *I* think Great-great-grandfather Spenser was just a forty-niner who happened to hit lucky way down in Nevada, and came back with some big ideas, like so many of them did. Anyway, I *feel* more like a forty-niner than an English poet."

John Lamb grinned. "You look more like one too. That outfit would've been a riot down on the Barbary Coast. The bacon smells wonderful, I think I'll have some too."

"I knew you would. That's why I cooked so much."

They ate at the table in front of the big studio window, from which, she assured him, there was the most fantastic view of the Bay. Fog coiled around the panes as if seeking a way in.

Remembering how her brother had said in the car, "You know what she's like," and how he had come to the conclusion that he knew very little, he now said, "Go on! Uncle Phew left it to your father; that doesn't explain how it comes to be yours."

"It would, if you knew Father. A house in San Francisco is the last thing *he* wants; he's too busy rushing around the Eastern Seaboard, throwing dead seabirds at the presidents of oil companies."

"He has a point."

"Oh sure. He's nice, and he's not just a weirdo, he's a professor of biology, so I guess he has a right to be fixated on the ecological thing. I doubt if you'll ever meet him. Richie managed to see him for a few minutes last year on his way to Europe, but I haven't seen him for five years. And Mother . . ." She gestured with a mushroom. Lamb had met Mrs. Charles Owen Spenser in Paris—a confirmed Francophile like himself and an almost compulsive traveler who returned to her native Boston as infrequently as possible; he understood that she had long since given up thinking about her husband, of whom she seemed retrospectively fond.

He said, "I don't see why you should be angry because your brother leased the place, if she's paying a decent rent."

"Decent! It's astronomical—trust Richie!"

"You can't want to live in it yourself, it's vast."

"That's not the point, Michael, it's mine too, and he should have asked . . ." Her voice trailed away; she was staring at the expression on John Lamb's face. "What's the matter?"

Naked, Lamb suddenly felt silly. He stood up from the table, went across to his open suitcase, and pulled a robe out of it.

"Johnny, what's the matter?"

First there had been uncertainty—a kind of instinctive fear, which he had subdued. Then there had been the unfortunate meeting with her brother, but that had been canceled out by the happiness of seeing her again, of making love to her again after all these weeks. From love-making they had descended to this plane of amusing and uncomplicated friendliness, of love perhaps, which had always been the firm basis of their relationship, right from the beginning. And now . . . He turned back to her, controlling his temper, and asked, evenly he hoped, "Why did you call me Michael?"

"I didn't."

"I assure you, you did. Who's Michael?"

"Johnny, will you please tell me what the hell you're talking about?"

"You said, 'That's not the point, Michael,' and I'm asking you who Michael is."

"It was a slip of the tongue. So what? I don't even know anybody called Michael."

With a rational edge of his mind he thought that it would have been pleasant if this situation had never arisen. But it had arisen, and because of it, things were now out of control. He said, "Well, at least it's not the Yugoslav, he was called Stefan."

Ellie's temper, he knew, was just as fierce as his own, but, alas, a great deal quicker to catch fire. Now she said, "That sounds to me as if you've been talking to my darling brother."

"If you'd come to the airport to meet me . . ."

"I told you, I didn't get your damned cable."

"If you'd given me the right address, if you'd even been at home, for Christ's sake . . ."

"Okay, I get it—Richie was jealous because I was out with his boyfriend. What did he say?"

"Why did you call me Michael?"

"Goddammit, I don't *know*. What did Richie say?"

There was a small pause—the pause granted by the gods to humans in case they should ever have enough sense to draw back from the abyss; they seldom do. John Lamb didn't. "He said you and Stefan were screwing."

"And you believed it!"

"Who's Michael?"

Ellie picked up the nearest thing, her plate, and threw it at him. From this point the entire situation declined rapidly.

For a time the stable yard echoed, but softly because of the fog, to raised voices, the slamming of doors, the wrenching open of doors, more raised voices, the slamming and locking of doors, voices, and eventual silence. To all this the yard listened attentively; the big house listened attentively; the people in the big house listened attentively. Later, the lights above the stable went out. Later still, the lights in the big house went out. Time passed. The fog blew cold and wild from the vast distances of the Pacific Ocean. The sound of the cuckoo clock, fog muffled, announced that the hour was two. Time passed.

Later, in the dead stillness of the small hours, a voice, a woman's voice, called softly in the big house: "Michael? Mikey?" And after a long, listening pause: "Michael?" But it seemed that there was no answer.

Three

ELLIE SAT at the table in the big window of the studio, drinking coffee and watching the age-old and endlessly fascinating morning battle of sun and fog. In the far corner of the room, in the big bed to which he had been readmitted at some unidentifiable hour before dawn, John Lamb slept soundly at last, readjusting himself to the nine hours' difference in time between Paris and San Francisco.

The studio had been built on top of the stables by Ellie's Grand-uncle Harold in 1919. This was the Harold whose Homeric rows with his brother, Owen, had delighted the city for many years until some particularly volcanic eruption had severed the family completely, dividing it henceforth into two never-to-be-confused parts. The Harold Spensers had stayed; the Owen Spensers had taken what was theirs, after a great deal of sub-rosa litigation (which had also delighted the city for many years) and had traveled East to set up house in Philadelphia, where, after a good deal of financial skirmishing, and a lot more social skirmishing, they had eventually been accepted as part of the local scene.

The very presence of Ellie, sitting at the window of *his* studio, was probably enough to set Harold Spenser spinning in his grave, let alone the fact that owing to a lapse in Harold Spenser fecundity the house now belonged to Ellie and her brother. The Owen Spensers had returned. The wheel had turned full circle. Or possibly, across eternity, Harold and Owen had long since joined hands in peace.

Local gossip in 1919 had guessed that Harold had built the studio in order to escape from his wife, Stella, younger than himself and mercilessly sociable. The truth was that he had built it because, like many another man born to money, he had wished to prove to himself that beyond the Companies and Trusts and Incorporations, there was in fact an individual called Harold; he had thought that he might prove this by releasing a hitherto repressed artistic talent. Proof of how wrong he was, unkindly making itself available long after he himself was dead, could still be found in various dark corners of the big house, indestructibly framed in heavy gold. Luckily, the studio also remained, a far better memorial to whatever of the artist had lurked in Harold.

John Lamb, waking slowly to a glitter of sunlight, sat up and could hardly believe his eyes. Beyond the wooded slopes of the Presidio, Mount Tamalpais lifted its soft curves to a pale clear sky; then swept down across Marin County to the Golden Gate and its breathtaking bridge; while away to the right, beyond Alcatraz, beyond that wide expanse of pale-blue water like an inverted sky, lay Tiburon, Angel Island, and the misty hills circling San Pablo Bay.

Ellie had not seen him sit up, so that in the moment before his exclamation of delighted surprise made her turn, he was aware of her as a disturbing silhouette against the bright vista of air and water; disturbing because there was no mistaking the pensive sadness of

her pose, elbow on table, chin cupped in palm, eyes on
her coffee cup. When she turned she smiled, but the
sadness persisted and haunted him all that laughing
day, so that when at last, towards evening, terror
appeared and confronted him face to face, he was in
some way not unprepared.

"I told you," she said, enjoying his astonished pleasure. "Isn't it like I said it was?"

He sat down opposite her, his eyes on the Bay; then
turned to her and smiled. For years he had been faithful
to Paris, and perhaps, however Paris might change and
whatever people might say of her, she would always be
his first love; but he had a suspicion that there was
about to be another city in his life.

Chattering like a child, delighting in his delight, Ellie
led him through what she called her "tourist day."
Lamb had always believed that any city worth loving
must not only be beautiful but full of interesting-
looking people, with a dash of eccentricity; San Francisco was well endowed with these virtues. He liked a
city to be capable of instant generosity, as well as of
reserving more secret and more intimate pleasures for
those who will love her more deeply; San Francisco
nobly met this qualification, spreading out her delights
with prodigality and good humor, so that the tourist
day became a grand and exhausting jumble of hilltop
vistas and Chinese grocery shops, of trolley-cars with
the climbing proclivities of mountain goats, of giant
crabs piled in steaming pyramids, and always of sky
and water, sunlight and distances girdled with more
hills.

On the day that they had first met, he had shown her
Paris in this way; and afterwards they had gone back to

his flat, carrying a meal of Quiche Lorraine and wine and fruit and cheese, to eat and to make love. So on this day, hand in hand and laughing as before, they went back to her studio, carrying a meal of cracked crab and wine and cheese and fruit, to eat and make love. If the argument of the night before had not been forgotten, neither had they allowed it to obtrude on their pleasure; and if, from time to time, he had recalled the sadness he had seen in her on waking, he had given no indication of it.

They paused in the stable yard with their packages, looking up, smiling, at the big house which towered above them. It was impossible not to smile at it. The first decade of the twentieth century, which had given birth to it, has never been remarkable for architectural taste, and some of the mansions built by San Franciscans to replace those destroyed by the disastrous earthquake and fire of April 1906 are prime examples of their period. Number 337 Gilman Street was a vast phantasmagoria of turrets and balconies and bulging bay-windows; the only two things which gave it any kind of cohesion were its overall absurdity and the fact that at some point in its history somebody had caused it to be painted a pleasing creamy white.

Smiling also, Ellie said, "I love it, I really do. I think Richie would quite like to sell it, but I'll never let him, never." She spoke fiercely, possessively, and John Lamb, even after one day in this city, understood it. He had noticed many signs of fierce possessiveness during that day and had found it an endearing quality and, in Western America, a rare one. The heights on which they stood were covered with such architectural absurdities, all of them enormous, all of them inhabited by rich people, and all of them very evidently cared for with devotion. It was a city which remembered its past with pride. Standing there, hand in hand with the girl he loved, Lamb could not know how deeply he was about to become involved in that past, nor in what devious ways—any more than he could know how closely they were again being examined by sharp eyes from one of the shadowy windows above them. But the time of his ignorance, his innocence, was running out fast now.

While they ate their crab and their cheese and their fruit, while they drank their wine, the last sands of this time trickled through the glass. And when at last he took her in his arms and began to kiss her, the glass was empty.

Later, going over and over and over the sequence of this love-making in his mind, he was unable to pinpoint the exact moment at which uneasiness had begun, yet he was sure that at some point before the final one there had been uneasiness at the back of his mind. He knew Ellie well; they had made love many times before; later he was to blame himself bitterly because his senses had been closed against warnings just as they had been closed against them in New York, on the plane, and during the early hours of his arrival; she had sat by the window, lost in a sadness he could not understand; she had called him Michael, and his suspicion had unleashed the worst argument they had ever had; yet, because he didn't want to disturb his own pleasure, he had not pursued either of these leads to their conclusion. Later, inevitably blaming himself, he imagined that it was this laziness in him which had permitted the whole terrible business to begin—and once begun, there was certainly no stopping it.

Later, however he might reassemble the pattern, he never succeeded in making sense of it. (He could not help remembering how once, in his youth, two very similar jigsaw puzzles had somehow become mixed together; he had never been able to sort them out; the memory of that frustration returned to him.) All that he knew for certain was that after he had achieved the sexual climax, and after Ellie had achieved it too—he was sure of that, though he grew less sure of it as time passed—she continued to writhe and moan beneath him.

At first, somewhat fatuously pleased (Jesus, what pompous, self-centered idiots men were!) that he had roused her to such passion, he held her tightly and continued to kiss her. Only as the seconds passed did he realize that there was something wrong. He raised his body, looking down at the loved face now contorted in what seemed to be an interminably prolonged sexual spasm. It was then that the fear started. In fear, he removed his body from hers altogether; she continued to writhe, whispering endearments. Suddenly it was obscene, and fear flowered into terror. He said something stupid, like "Ellie? Ellie, stop it!" And, "Ellie, look at me!"—because her eyes were closed. She continued to writhe.

His brain was not working properly; it was stumbling and sliding down the steep hill of his terror, out of control. He went after it and grabbed it, and somehow brought it to a stop. The first thing he did, because what he was witnessing did seem to him like some kind of hysteria, was to try slapping her face—gently at first, because he loved her, then not so gently because she terrified him. It had no effect. He covered her squirming nakedness, which had suddenly lost all its beauty, all its innocence, but she flung the sheet away from her, gasping.

Returning intelligence brought with it some useless snippet of knowledge gleaned from somewhere: in certain extreme conditions it was possible—wasn't it?—for sensual titillation to produce a kind of hypnotic reaction—yes, a kind of amnesia. So then he thought immediately, Get a doctor! It was not an action he relished—not a situation that called for very much publicity—yet he could see no way out of it. Of course, if he sat by her and waited, there was every chance that the spasm, whatever it might be, would wear itself out. He went back to the bed and looked at her; nothing had changed; the loved face was still oddly contorted; there was a terrible tension evidenced in every line of the loved body; the neck tendons were taut, the hands white-knuckled with strain, grasping handfuls of sheet and tearing at them strongly; sweat shone all over the fine fair skin.

No, he could not wait; he could not know if, in waiting, he might be causing her some harm, some lasting harm. Then it had to be a doctor—but not any doctor, *her* doctor.

He ran across the big room to the telephone. The dark-red address book with her name embossed on it in gold—which he had first seen in Paris and knew so well—lay beside it. But, as he very soon found, there was no doctor listed in it. He remembered that some-where, in some Parisian restaurant, she had said, "Oh, we're disgustingly healthy, we Owen Spensers, we're *never* sick." He could remember her exact expression, so funny and so dear, as she said it; he could even remember a yellow curtain with a tasseled fringe which had been behind her head—and the Nouveau Beaujolais had just made its yearly appearance. He was about to throw the address book down when one of the names he had glimpsed in it returned to him—perhaps the only name in all its pages that he could have possibly recognized: "Richie."

The idea of contacting her brother did not appeal to him at all; he could only guess that Ellie would have been enraged by it. On the other hand, he *was* her brother, and if he didn't know the name of her doctor, he would certainly know the name of *a* doctor who would be trustworthy. He made up his mind, which was now operating normally, found the number and dialed it.

Richard Owen Spenser's voice said, "San Francisco Fire Department, can I help you?"

"Richard? This is John Lamb. Listen to me—Ellie needs a doctor. I can't find one listed in her address book."

Homosexuals were a constant source of surprise to him. He had expected all kinds of questions and quibbles and other skittishness, but Richard simply said, "She doesn't have one, not one of her own. You'd better call Hillier, he's kind of the family quack. I'll give you his number . . ."

Lamb could hear pages being turned. Ellie continued to twist this way and that on the bed, gasping and moaning.

Richard supplied the number, and added, "I'll be right over."

"There's no need." It was instinctive.

"Don't be silly! A—She's never sick. B—If it wasn't serious, she'd call herself. C—I *am* her brother, not just a good lay she picked up in Paris. D—You're scared, and therefore so am I." With which he replaced his receiver, cutting the connection.

It did not seem right for three men to stand around the bed looking at her. Richard had gone to the window, where he stood very still, staring out at the myriad glittering lights surrounding the Bay. Lamb hovered in the middle of the room, wanting to be with her but not wanting to have to witness her agony. The doctor sat on a chair by the bed; he had taken her pulse, checked her blood pressure, and guessed that there was no actual fever; now he regarded her intently, frowning. He was a pleasant fresh-faced man of forty-five; it amused him that he looked more like a sailor than a family doctor—because sailing was his passion, and the ills, both real and imaginary, of his rich patients interested him far less than did the mystique of tack and spinnaker. He knew that there was a standing joke among at least one group of his patients: "Make sure you never get sick on a fine day with a fresh wind blowing!"; but he also knew that they liked him as a doctor, or he would long ago have been out of a job, even if his name *was* Hillier. (There had been Hilliers around ever since the old days of South Place and Rincon Hill.)

There were also occasions—and this was one of them—when the old excitement, the old driving curiosity which he could remember so well from the days of his youth, returned to him. Gazing at the beautiful girl in the grip of whatever possessed her (and he had no idea what that might be), he was a student again; the mystery of life meant more to him once more than did the mystery of wind and water—an increasingly rare occurrence.

He turned and looked at the two young men who hovered in the big shadowy room behind him, then stood up and moved to join them. They both stared at him with what he took to be expressions of hope and trust; this pained him because he knew he was going to do nothing to earn hope or trust; inevitably, he was going to lie to them. He said, "Don't expect me to tell you what's the matter with her, I don't know. Some kind of psychosomatic condition induced by the sex-act, which is about the most violent psychosomatic experience the average human being ever undergoes— except being born, I guess—dying maybe."

Glancing towards her with distaste, Richard said, "Can't you give her a shot—something like that?"

"Oh sure. There's a dozen things I could give her, but I kind of like the old rule: diagnose before you prescribe." He scratched his neatly cut greying hair—a seaman's cut, nothing to get in the eyes at a crucial moment. The eyes themselves were grey also; they regarded the two stricken young faces analytically; he smiled. "One thing I *can* prescribe is three strong Scotches."

Richard went into the kitchen. The doctor looked at John Lamb. "Embarrassing for you. I wouldn't like to say it could happen to anybody, but I guess it could."

"Isn't there . . . anything you can do to stop it? I mean, it's . . . over half an hour now, it must be using up every bit of energy she has."

"Yes, it is."

"That can't be good for her."

"Hard to say. Physical exhaustion itself may stop it—she's as strong as a horse. You never . . . noticed anything like it before?"

"Good God, no."

"Not necessarily in connection with sex. Any aberration, any oddity, here or in Paris."

Richard returned with Scotch, ice, water, glasses. Lamb thought of the "Michael" incident and dismissed it. In retrospect he found his behavior on that occasion reprehensible and, worse, unfeeling. How many times had his own tongue slipped into calling a person by another name? He said, "No, nothing."

Pouring whiskey, Richard said, "I noticed something —something pretty odd." He glanced at Lamb. "That's why I insisted on coming over right away when you called." He gave them their drinks, and stood staring into the clear amber of his glass for a moment, deep in thought. "It happened the first time we met after she got back from this trip to Europe. It couldn't have been called anybody's favorite reunion; in fact, we had one hell of a fight. You probably know that I leased the house while she was away, without asking her. I tried her Paris number a couple of times, but she wasn't home. She'd"—eying Lamb—"changed her address, if you know what I mean.

"Anyway, I was afraid I'd lose this female—Jesus, it's not just anybody who wants to lease thirteen bedrooms this time of year, *and* pay for it in advance. So I closed the deal, and Ellie was mad at me, God knows why!

"So here we were in the middle of this fight, no holds

barred, and I was making some kind of a speech—I forget what it was about, but I know it ended in a question. Maybe I said, 'What the hell would you have done in my place?' something like that; and she didn't answer. So then I repeated it, and she still didn't say anything. She was standing about here."

The other two men watched him gravely as he went towards the window.

"She was unpacking at the time—books, I guess—and when she didn't answer the second time, I looked at her . . . you know, pretty closely. She was staring at the front door, and something about the way she was standing struck me as . . . weird—as though she was listening to something. Well, I'll tell you, if she was, *I* couldn't hear it!

"Anyway, then I went real close to her; I guess maybe I said something, I don't remember, the whole thing was so creepy. She was miles away, she wasn't even hearing me. She was standing right here in the middle of this goddam shouting-match, staring at the door like a zombie—zonked! I tell you, it scared the shit out of me.

"After a while, kind of . . . you know, gently, I touched her arm; and as soon as I did that she turned and looked at me. She was surprised; I mean it, really surprised, but I think she half-knew something pretty strange had happened."

Hillier nodded. "You told her? You discussed it with her?"

"Sure. She acted as if she didn't believe me. Or—" He broke off, looking unhappy, and took a gulp of his whiskey. "Jesus, this may just be guessing, but I got the idea she *did* believe me, and it scared her too, and she didn't want to talk about it."

"And all you did was touch her arm?"

"That's all."

The doctor nodded again and was silent for a time. Lamb noticed that his expression had closed in an odd way; he put this down to thought; later he was to think otherwise. Eventually, Hillier said, "Okay. Nine doctors out of ten would have called in some kind of psychiatric specialist fifteen minutes ago. For better or worse, not worse I hope, I'm the tenth—because I've had cases where the psychiatrist has done more harm than good.

"My guess is that when Ellie comes out of this she'll know that *something* happened, but she won't know what and she won't know why; and I suggest that the two of you keep it that way as near as you can. A head-shrinker is going to open up so many cans of peas that in a week or two that nice, beautiful, and above all, *healthy* girl over there is going to imagine she's some kind of nut-case."

Richard was giving the doctor an unusually cool, straight, and ice-blue look; he opened his mouth to say something, glanced at John Lamb, and shut it again.

"Now," said Hillier, "we're going to try to get her out of it. That means you, Richie." And because Lamb also moved, instinctively, he added, "No, not you—you're the last person we want touching her."

Lamb stayed where he was; he could feel the blood mounting to his face. Nervously, Richard said, "Jesus, I'm no good at this kind of thing. I never even hold their heads when they vomit, I just lock the bathroom door on them."

"However, you brought her out of whatever it was before by simply touching her arm."

"Sure, but that was different." He looked down, round-eyed, at the shuddering sweat-bathed female body on the ravaged bed. "What . . . are we going to do, for God's sake?"

"Well—it used to be called 'the laying on of hands.' "

Ellie's brother looked at him as if he were a madman.

"I'm going to hold her still—as still as I can. I want you to touch her, speak to her, kiss her maybe, I don't know. This is a few thousand years old, I wasn't around when they invented it."

Moving with sudden surprising speed and strength, he grasped the shuddering body by the forearms, pinning them to her sides. The mouth gaped and let out a strangled cry. Richard hesitated, appalled. The doctor, who was quite obviously using most of his strength, hissed, "Oh for Christ's sake, Richie, go *on!*"

With a palpable effort of will, for which Lamb admired him greatly, Richard bent forward, putting his hands on each side of his sister's distorted face. As soon as they touched this flesh, which was also his flesh, he seemed to know instinctively what to do; the fingers held the head still, firmly and gently, and then began to caress the cheeks, up and down. He said, "Ellie? Ell, it's me, it's Richie." He must have felt or sensed some reaction, because suddenly the tension, the aversion seemed to leave him. He dropped on his knees beside the bed and leaned right over, resting his face against hers. From where he stood, John Lamb could see the two faces quite clearly for a moment, so akin, the one very cool and calm now, the other sweaty and agonized. Then Richard turned, so that his features were hidden against her neck; he threw an arm across the wet shoulders, holding her tightly against him; he kept saying, "Ell? Ell, it's me, it's Richie . . ."

For a long minute this extraordinary tableau continued. The grey-haired doctor kneeling over her, making sure that he touched her only with his hands, making sure that those hands were merely a human vise, taking care that his touch should not be that of a man—and her brother, who was not quite a man, holding her against him in that embrace which was so instinct with love that Lamb, who was after all responsible for her condition, felt ashamed of himself. Then, quite quickly, almost miraculously, the torment ebbed out of her and she lay still. The doctor released her instantly and got off the bed; it took her brother longer to realize that he had accomplished whatever task it was that had been demanded of him. He released her more slowly, and sat back on his heels, looking at the calm now-recognizable face with astonishment. When he stood up, they could see that his cheeks were wet with tears. He went past them into the bathroom and closed the door. The doctor said, "*Now* I can give her a shot."

An hour later Ellie lay soundly, placidly asleep on a turned mattress between clean sheets. John Lamb and Richard, feeling a great deal better after a large Scotch and a stick of marijuana, respectively, were on the point of saying good night. Dr. Hillier's final instruction had been that the girl was not to be disturbed in any way until her natural exhaustion or the shot he had given her, whichever lasted longer, had worn off and she awoke naturally; he added that this might not be until well after noon.

Richard said, "What did you think of Hillier?"

"I thought he was good. I liked him." Richard stared at the tip of his reefer and said nothing. "I take it you *don't* like him."

"I'm not sure. He's one of the old crowd, you know; they're too darn busy protecting their own interests, I guess I never *quite* believe what they say."

Liking him, Lamb said, "You love her a lot, don't you? Nobody would have guessed it from what you said yesterday."

Richard looked at his sister's recumbent form, but in his expression lingered the memory of that other girl, because that's what she had seemed to be, who had lain there writhing and whimpering so obscenely. "I guess we're pretty close," he said. "The kind of parents we have, it's not so very surprising, is it?" He looked back at Lamb, his blue eyes hard. "You heard what the doc said—you won't go . . . touching her."

"You have to be joking. As if I would!"

"I get the feeling you're kind of a horny guy."

"Not unusually so, I assure you."

Richard laughed softly. "Jesus, I get quite a bang out of you, maybe it wouldn't be so bad having you for a brother-in-law, after all." He turned to go; then looked back. "Call me after Hillier's been in the morning, huh? I'd like to know what he says."

"Of course."

At the door he paused, frowning. "There's something I forgot to tell him—I don't know whether it matters or not. It was during that same fight, over me leasing the house without asking her. I guess it's something everybody does from time to time, but somehow . . . with her own brother . . ."

John Lamb's stomach contracted. He knew with absolute certainty what was coming, and his face must have revealed the thought, because Richard took a pace back into the room, looking at him more closely. "What's the matter?"

Lamb swallowed and said, "She . . . she called you by another name. Right?"

It was Richard's turn to stare. "You too?"

John Lamb nodded.

"Michael?"

John Lamb nodded again.

Four

WHILE ELLIE slept, long into another sparkling day, John Lamb sat at the table in the window and wrote:

Dear Jean-Paul,

I hope all goes well with you and Martine. I must say, it's a wonderful feeling to be able to go away and know that I needn't have any worry at all about the business.

I only stopped in New York for two nights on my way here, but I managed to talk to four or five of the people we discussed, including Steiner, who is very bright indeed. As you know, I plan to spend a week there on my way back to Paris, and I'll naturally get a more detailed picture then.

Steiner's opinion is that from the architect/designer aspect of our business we'd be stupid to stick our necks out across the Atlantic. Whatever one may think of their work (and Steiner agrees with us) there are already far too many decorators in America. However, it really does look as though there may be an interesting market here for our antique department—not at the highest price-levels, which are as you know very high indeed in this rich country, but at some lower price range which would tempt the more sophisticated young marrieds. Steiner emphasised that the stuff would have to be *antique* and of good quality, making it a sensible minor investment for the buyer. There is an enormous amount of reproduction junk on the market here, and as much forged antique junk as well; at least, that's what I suspect.

I think that if I can persuade Steiner to come in with us on a workable basis, his reputation here combined with ours in Europe could add up to a specialized but profitable extension of Duvallet-Lamb et Cie.

Steiner agreed that New York is the place to start, but he urged me to pay a quick visit to Dallas or Houston if I could manage it, since they are apparently . . .

He was suddenly aware of the fact that Ellie had woken up; she had raised herself on the pillows and was regarding him intently as he wrote. He stood up and went over to her quickly, tenderness and a cowardly dread contending inside him. She turned into his arms gratefully, burying her face against him, holding him very tightly. Understanding flowed between them, as it always did; he realized that to some degree she was aware of what she had undergone.

Her voice muffled, she said, "Oh, Johnny, what happened? What did I do?"

There was something odd about the second part of this question, but he was too busy trying to recall Dr. Hillier's instructions to notice it. "There's nothing to worry about."

"But look at the *time*, it's after two."

"Darling, I'm sorry—I had to send for a doctor, he . . ."

"*Doctor!* What doctor?" Horrified, as he had known she would be.

"Hillier. He gave you a shot." Then, with his arms close about her, he told her the prepared story: a certain kind of overstimulation of the nervous system arising from sexual intercourse—a kind of hypnotic-hysterical reaction, which had scared him into calling

Richie—hence Dr. Hillier—nothing to worry about—rest and the avoidance of any kind of stimulation for a few days. As he spoke he could feel her body reacting to everything he said, but he made it long and ordinary; he even tried to make it boring; and before he had finished she had leaned back in his arms and was staring up at him, her blue eyes thoughtful. What her thoughts were she did not say. When he had finished she was silent for a long time, her cool fingers moving absently on his neck and hair. At last—lightly, because he needed to hide his fear—he said, "I don't suppose you remember a thing, do you?" He could have wished that she had answered at once in the negative, but she did not do this. She looked up at him again, searching his face tenderly; only then, and after what seemed a very long time, did she say, "No, not a thing," and he knew that she had given the answer that she knew he wanted to hear. He was profoundly unsettled.

After that she agreed with unusual docility that of course he must call Dr. Hillier; she greeted the doctor as if he were a member of her favorite profession instead of one she all but despised, and she submitted to his examination calmly, accepting without question his prescription of a mild sedative to be taken three times a day, and a stronger one at night. John Lamb's uneasiness deepened.

Dr. Hillier may have been aware of her true feeling about his calling, from bitter past experience perhaps, because he did not draw Lamb aside for the usual post-examinatory quiet word; he headed straight for the front door, and there, on shaking hands, strengthened the pressure of his fingers for an instant and merely said, "You have my number if you need me."

The younger man thought that he looked a trifle distrait; this was indeed the case; tomorrow was Sunday, and all Robert Hillier's thoughts were concentrated on the wish—the itching, driving desire—for a sunny day and a strong steady wind; he could almost feel the deck of his beloved *Juanita* bucking beneath his feet.

Ellie, after his departure, was inclined to be merry, and though he loved her in this mood, John Lamb could not dismiss that uneasiness from his mind; neither could he dismiss the idea that the uneasiness itself was petty and unworthy. The girl he loved had passed through a terrifying and inexplicable ordeal; she had emerged from it in high good spirits, apparently—even the merriment itself was slightly suspect—and all *he* could do was feel uneasy. He sensed the same kind of dissatisfaction in her brother when he called for a report on her condition; they obviously shared an unspoken opinion that too many questions remained unanswered.

In the meantime, Ellie insisted on being taken out to dinner. She put on her favorite Parisian dress because, she assured him, the restaurant to which he was taking her really was more than a little like Paris. And indeed, much to his surprise, this turned out to be true; the place was owned by Frenchmen and largely staffed by them, rare enough in any "French" establishment outside France, but then, as he was beginning to understand, San Francisco was a rare place, with a true pride in itself and a true individuality which other cities (his own native London, alas, among them) were fast losing or had already lost.

Naturally, the Frenchmen were delighted to speak

French, which Lamb, being born a cockney, handled slightly better than he handled English.

He and Ellie were very close to each other that evening, very aware of their love—perhaps, ironically, because the actual act of love had been put temporarily beyond their reach by doctor's orders—and very aware of the depths across which they had perilously skated on the thinnest of thin ice. The unanswered questions remained unanswered, it was true, but under the influence of love, good food, and wine, John Lamb found that he could almost forget them. Which was why, towards the end of the meal, he leaned forward, taking both her warm soft hands between his own, and said, "Now, Miss Eleanor Owen Spenser, please listen attentively because this is very important. I'm going to stay in this marvelous city two weeks; then I'm going back to Paris, via Dallas, Texas, and I want you to come with me. We'll enter into a state of Holy Deadlock at any whistle stop along the way you care to choose." And, since Ellie looked down at her coffee cup and said nothing: "I'd better warn you that this is the third time of asking, and you may never be offered the chance again."

To his horror he saw two large tears well out from under the down-turned lashes. In a stifled voice, Ellie said, "Oh Jesus Christ, why did you have to . . . to say it here?"

For a moment he was stunned; then, aided by a good deal of Gallic and San Franciscan tact, managed to make excuses, pay the bill, and get her out of the place.

At some later moment in time (five minutes? half an hour?) they appeared to be sitting side by side on a hard, cold seat in Huntington Park, his arm around her

still-shuddering shoulders. Obviously, his earlier prescience had not been misinformed; he had been right to
sense a falsehood, lying cold and hard somewhere at
the heart of her assumed gaiety.

After a long time she said, "I'm so . . . sorry. It was
just . . . you took me by surprise. Oh, I do love you,
Johnny—I love you so *much!*" The blue eyes were
fierce.

"That's all I want to hear. Nothing else matters."

She shook her head, the frank fierce eyes fixed on his
face. "A lot of other things matter. I guess . . . I guess
I'm an idiot, I thought I could fool you, I thought I could
keep it up the way it is now, until the time came for you
to go. And then . . ." She glanced away, unable to
meet his amazed brown stare. "And then I could just be
vague—you know how good I am at being vague; and
you'd go, and somehow it would . . . kind of fizzle out
there."

"Will you please tell me what the hell you're talking
about?"

Still not looking at him, she said, "I . . . I can't marry
you, Johnny, don't you see that?"

Between fury and laughter, because it really did seem
to him both infuriating and absurd, he said, "No, I don't
see it at all. See *what,* for Christ's sake?"

Looking at the softly lit rose window of Grace
Cathedral, Ellie replied, "I wasn't sure but I am now.
There's insanity in our family."

He refused to accept it, either then or later. Right or
wrong, stupid or not, reasonable or unreasonable, some
native pigheadedness rose up in him and made him
lash out furiously at every aspect of this unthinkable

idea. He had known that he loved her, of course, but the fierce unreasoning strength of that love had never struck him until this moment, and he realized, instinctively and at once, that the true danger lay not in his acceptance but in hers.

This first argument, fraught with fears and pitfalls, carried them from Huntington Park to the car, back to the park, where she had dropped her purse, back to the car, and eventually back to the studio.

"I never heard anything so absurd. Just because you had some perfectly ordinary kind of nervous upset . . ." But he knew that it was not perfectly ordinary, and he was afraid.

"It's not that—not just that. Oh Johnny, don't make it any more difficult than it is."

"I intend to make it as difficult as I bloody well can. You've been ill, for about the first time in your healthy little life, and it's upset you."

"There are other things. I wouldn't say it just because of that. Oh Jesus, I know—don't you see that. I *know!*"

"What do you know?"

"Please, please don't ask me—not now."

"Why not now? Ellie, I won't accept it, I just won't."

They drove in silence, pitching up and over San Francisco's absurd street intersections—pitching down and over them. He had taken the wheel of her car without asking her; she was demonstrably in no condition to drive. Her voice trembling, she said, "Look . . . Look at Father! Look at the way he . . . he behaves! Do you call that normal? Nobody else does."

"Your father's fanatically concerned with the mess

we've made of our ecology, and there's nothing even remotely insane about that."

"Richie's abnormal."

"He's queer—the jury's still out on that one. Otherwise he can run rings around most so-called normal people, he's as bright as a button."

Pacing nervously to and fro in her big beautiful room, she came, at last, down to the root of the matter. "You never met Uncle Hugh—the one who died last year and left the house to Father. There . . . There was a terrible scandal about six years ago—they . . . caught him with some little girl, it was ghastly."

"Child molesting is a sexual deviation; it's abnormal but it's not insane—and it doesn't run in families." He didn't like bullying her, but he really did feel that he could see light at the end of the tunnel; she had been brooding alone over family idiosyncrasies, and there wasn't a family in the world that couldn't, if it tried, produce a few prime examples of its own.

She stopped her pacing and stood face to face with him. "One of his sisters, Aunt Leona—they had to lock her up. Johnny, please look at me! *She was certified and put away.*"

He felt like asking her if she was sure, but could tell at a glance that she was—or thought she was; he could very easily check on Aunt Leona. All he could think of saying at the moment was, "Okay, so you have a mildly kooky family. It happens. So have most people, so have I. Mine doesn't affect me, and yours needn't affect you— You're tired out, I'm going to put you to bed with one of Hillier's pink pills."

He moved, but she held his arm, her face strained

and white. "Johnny—that . . . thing that happened last night. It wasn't the first time."

He felt fear run its chill fingers up his spine.

"Early last week, Richie . . . came over to see me with his boyfriend . . ." He didn't want to listen to this, but her bleak face and the pain in her beautiful eyes held him fast. "We sat around and talked, and then suddenly it was getting dark, so I asked them to dinner . . . only . . . you know me, there wasn't a thing to eat. Well, Richie's a far better cook than I am—he really is a marvelous cook—so he said he'd go down to the market and get a few things, and cook us a meal: mussaka, he makes a terrific mussaka. So off he went, leaving me to cope with Stefan. You've met Stefan, he's okay but he's kind of sticky, he doesn't talk much English . . ." She searched his face for a moment in silence; then turned away to the window. Lamb stayed exactly where she had held him, transfixed. He thought he could discern the rough shape of what was coming towards him, and didn't want to see it any more clearly.

Ellie said, "You can believe this or not, as you like—but I don't find Stefan at all attractive. Maybe it's because I . . . kind of sense the bisexual thing in him—or maybe it's just because he's my brother's boyfriend—but anyway, I never have liked men who . . . kind of purr over their own good looks, that's why Italians turn me right off." She wheeled around and looked at him; her eyes were wild now, the pupils slightly enlarged. The sight of them made his heart pound violently; this time fear dragged its sharp finger-nails across his spine.

"I don't like him, Johnny, I don't find him attractive —but . . . I can't explain it—I can't say that *I* knew that I was going to have him, because in a way it wasn't me making the decision. It seemed to come . . . Yes it did, it seemed to come from outside me. But what difference does that make? It was me that went for him like . . . like a bitch in heat, it was me that pulled his pants open . . ." Tears were pouring down her cheeks again. Pointing furiously, she gasped, "I had him, I had that stupid hunk of lard right there on that bed; it makes me *sick* when I think of it."

John Lamb, remembering the agonized naked figure which had writhed on that bed only a few hours before, felt sick himself—not with disgust, though he would have been less than human if disgust had not moved in his stomach at some point during her story, but sick with bewilderment and fear and anger. Uppermost in his mind, however, was a very pure and innocent surprise, because for the first time in his life he was realizing that yet another hoary old maxim was vividly and actually true: love does, in fact, conquer all. He was devastated, not by the horror and obscenity of what she had told him, but by a great wave of tenderness which pushed him violently towards her and threw his arms around her. Clinging to him, she gasped, "You see? You *see?*"

He could hardly believe that it was his own voice, so calm, which replied, "I see that you're absolutely exhausted. I see that I was a nincompoop ever to have taken you out on the town this evening. Yes—and I see that we're going to have to check on a couple of things so that we can kick this sick little idea right out of your head."

"But Johnny, you can't want me after what I've just said. Jesus, I may be some . . . some kind of nymphomaniac. You'd better go right back to Paris before you—"

"Don't," Lamb said, "talk such balls!" Even as he spoke out of that love and tenderness, he was aware of the thin wire across the abyss on which they were both balanced. Whether she had imagined the incident with Stefan (as he was inclined to believe), or whether it had actually happened, there was sickness in it somewhere. Not insanity, he would never accept that, but sickness which had to be cured. He would have liked to go to see Dr. Hillier at that very moment, but not only was it now nearly midnight and therefore too late, he had no intention of leaving her alone with her wild thoughts and her misery.

He looked down at her. She was still clutching him tightly, her cheek pressed into his chest; her eyes were closed, the delicate lashes, which she refused to mutilate with makeup, wet with tears. He said, "Now look, let's be sensible, we usually are. What do you do with a kid when he thinks there's a hairy man with a knife in the closet under the stairs? You take him there and you open the closet and you show him that there's no one there at all, and what's more, there's no *room* for anyone. And that's just what we're going to have to do with this bogeyman of yours . . ."

"You think it's that easy?" The note of bitterness was not lost on him.

"No, not easy—but possible, very easily possible."

She looked up at him then, frowning, as if his calmness and determination surprised her as much as it surprised him. He said, "Come on, get that dress off, I'm putting you to bed."

To his amazement, she raised no objection to Dr.

Hillier's bedtime pills, so he gave her two with some hot milk; then lay down with his arms around her and held her quietly, forbidding any more talk, until, surprisingly quickly, she slipped into drugged and exhausted slumber.

His own night, whether waking or sleeping, was a nightmare. Questions, which he could not answer anyway, kept him awake, and then, during the few fretful hours when he managed to sleep, pursued him into his dreams, entwining themselves with fantasy figures: Uncle Hugh leering after little girls—Aunt Leona (a pale, lined facsimile of Ellie herself) peering from behind bars—Stefan, all too real this figure, falling with surprised pleasure upon a slim and willing body which was, and was not, Ellie. So the raging argument of that first night, arising from her brother's suspicion, had really been a product of guilt. Why, if all that she had said was true, had she submitted to that desire for a young man she didn't even find attractive? Why had she never told her brother that he, John Lamb, wanted to marry her? What had caused her to pause, "like a zombie," lost to reality until her brother's touch had recalled her? Why had she called both of them "Michael"—the two men nearest to her, whose names were a part of her own being? Was it true that she knew no Michael? Then who was this Michael she didn't know?

Towards dawn, though he would still not entertain for one second any idea of insanity, he was driven to accept the common thread which ran all through this jumbled nightmare tapestry: the fact that all of it, every single aspect of it, sprang from Ellie's mind. Everything that haunted him, whether it was true or not (more terrifyingly if it was false), was lodged somewhere behind that beautiful uncomplicated forehead, within that shapely head with its cap of fine silky curls. And this itself was the biggest question mark of all—because in Paris, where they had known each other so very well, so intimately, for five crowded months, there had never once been any indication of any of these nightmares. Why in San Francisco and not in Paris?

Towards dawn he must have fallen once again into restless sleep. When he emerged from it, dry-mouthed and aching, it was to full daylight; he had forgotten to close the curtains. He did this now, quietly, so as not to wake Ellie, who slept contentedly on her side, one hand, half curled, lying childlike on the pillow beside her face. Fog blanketed the lower levels of the city. The marina was invisible, but the treetops of the Presidio arose from wreathing mist like a Japanese painting, as did the surprising red tower-tops of the bridge. He turned from them and looked down at the loved and sleeping face. It was strange, he thought—or perhaps not strange, because in a way unnecessary—that they had not, last night, referred once to the crux of the argument. In Paris, in the Louvre, standing in front of some heroic complication by Delacroix, she had suddenly said, "About getting married . . ." He had turned to her. "You want babies, don't you, I could never marry a man who didn't want babies."

Yes, he wanted babies, and by God he would have them, and what's more he would have them with this girl, and nothing, but *nothing*—not all the bogeymen and horror tales in the world—was going to stop him.

He went into the bathroom, washed and shaved without making any noise, left a note for her, saying that he had gone for a walk (in case she should wake before he returned, which looked very doubtful), consulted the telephone directory for the address, took her car, and presented himself at Dr. Hillier's house just as that zealous sailor was setting out to prepare his *Juanita* for what promised to be, within an hour, a perfect day for sailing.

Dr. Hillier was not pleased, but managed not to show it too plainly. His clothing, and the fact that it was eight o'clock on a Sunday morning, explained more succinctly than words could have done that this was his day off and that he planned to spend it in a specific way. He escorted Lamb into his den. (The house, hardly less surprising than 337 Gilman Street, appeared to be the bastard offspring of a Swiss chalet and an Elizabethan manor.) His coffeepot was still hot; he gave the Englishman a cup and took another for himself while he listened.

Lamb told him everything. He had been impressed by the way he had handled the problem which Ellie had presented two nights before, and as a young man who was never in need of a doctor, he had great faith in the medical profession; moreover, he badly needed to talk to *somebody*.

The only part of the story which caused Hillier to flash him a startled look was that concerning Stefan. Though he said nothing by way of corroboration, Lamb received the very definite impression that Aunt Leona and Uncle Hugh came as no surprise to him. The fact that Ellie had called both her brother and her lover by a name which, she claimed, meant nothing to her at all caused Hillier to grimace out of the window. Lamb had no way of telling what this grimace might mean.

He also had no way of telling just how ominous, in some ways even dangerous, his story seemed to the man who was listening to it. For a start, his family association with San Francisco had not started, back in the late 1850's, in a mansion on Rincon Hill a few doors away from the mansion built by "Old Dick" Spenser with a part of the spoils he had brought back in triumph from Nevada; his family had not moved from Rincon Hill, when the sprawling rumbustuous city had surrounded it, to build themselves another house on Bush Street in one of the magnificent "rows" of that time, and not a stone's throw from the Spenser house on Sutter; he had not been born in a house here on the Heights, to which the Hilliers, the Spensers, and their like had moved after the earthquake and fire of 1906. There was also, if Robert Hillier's memory served him right, the name Bellfort to be considered—just another name to this young foreigner, no doubt, but to Hillier and to any other knowledgeable member of the community, it had the sound of thunder: the thunder which rumbles on Mount Olympus.

When John Lamb had finished, the doctor sighed. He had no intention of saying anything now which he might regret, perhaps to his cost, later. The whole matter needed a great deal of thought—careful consideration; and there was no doubt at all that the proper place for thought and consideration was a sun-warmed seat in the stern of a well-trimmed sailing boat with the tiller tucked comfortably under your arm. That was incontrovertible. However, the anguish of this pleasant young man who stood facing him was also incontrovertible and had to be dealt with kindly—kindly but with extreme caution. (Where was Godfrey Bellfort living out his declining years anyway? In Rome—or had he sold that vast barn of a place? Marrakesh? The Bahamas?)

He said, "Well now—you're going to have to let me think about all this. In the first place, it's way, way outside my field . . ."

John Lamb was no fool. Ellie had told him enough about this town, and about the social section of it to which she belonged, for him to realize that Hillier was giving him the cool and cautious treatment; he accepted that and, in a way, admired it. He didn't have to say that the whole thing must be kept, as it were, in the family—on Pacific Heights, as on Rincon Hill, that was taken for granted. But he did say, "I was hoping you might be able to deal with it yourself. I don't like head-shrinkers any more than you do, and the fewer people who know about this . . ." He was sure that he could afford to leave that one in midair.

Hillier nodded absently, trying not to notice that the fog had now practically cleared. He said, "I dimly remember something about the aunt who lives in a . . . rest home—I never dealt with the case myself, but of course I can check on it. And poor old Hugh . . . Well, that's true enough, a most unfortunate business."

Sun, striking clear through the fog, forced him to action. Using his most decisive voice, he said, "All right, I get the picture. Leave it to me, I'll try to think up a way of dealing with it. There are a couple of opinions I can consult tomorrow morning—the kind who won't ask for specific details if I don't offer them.

Leave it to me, eh? Keep her quiet and don't let her brood on it."

With these words, which sounded even to him as empty as they undoubtedly were, he fled to freedom and open water. But even as he did so, an unpleasant itch somewhere in the recesses of his brain told him that in some way, which he would only come to appreciate later, a fine day's sailing was already ruined.

Ellie was awake when he returned to the studio. She had drawn back the curtains and now lay propped up in bed staring at the sparkling vista of sun and water and the last wisps of wreathing mist. She had not regained her natural color, and there was about her face a kind of lumpishness, a lumpish obstinacy of expression which, if the situation had been different, might have caused him certain qualms about their future life together. As things were, she was so patently unwell that the thought never entered his mind. The blue eyes, turned towards him, had no brilliance; neither had the smile, which did not come from the heart.

This was an Ellie he had never seen before, and he suspected that it was one she had never seen herself. He knew, from Parisian experience, that she had a mercurial temper with a low flash-point, but as with others of this type that he had met, the instant explosion acted as a safety valve against moods and sulks and other unlovable manifestations of the human spirit.

He made tea and toast for her; it took him some minutes. When he went back into the big room, carrying the tray, she was in exactly the same position, inert, lackluster eyes still fixed on the magnificent view but not, he suspected, seeing it. And this was his Ellie, who, except in sleep, was never absolutely still for more than a few seconds. She said, "My poor darling, am I a pain in the ass?"

He kissed her lightly and told her that she was the most beautiful pain in the ass the world had ever seen—but his uneasiness deepened. She said, "I'm bushed. I think I'll be a slut and stay in bed—would that be awful?"

"No, it'd be very sensible."

She tried a smile; tried a flash of the old spirit: "If this is being sick, being looked after like this, I guess I could grow to like it." He, too, smiled, but that uneasiness deepened again. Perhaps she sensed it; she said, "How to lose your man in one easy lesson, by El-e-a-nor Owen Spenser. What will *you* do with yourself all day?"

"I'd planned a little research into the history of your allegedly lunatic family—where do you suggest I start?"

"You have to be kidding."

"No, I mean it."

"Jesus! I know people have written things about them, I can't imagine why. *I* don't have anything here."

He had thought about this subject during the long hours of his sleepless night. "There must be a lot of stuff over there in the house."

"I guess. I never looked. Richie might know."

"Why don't I just go over and ask? You could call your lodgers and tell them to expect me—tell them I'm a friend."

Ellie tried another, not very successful smile and

reached for his hand. "You are gorgeous, and I really would love to marry you, it'd be such . . . such a *rest,* having somebody practical around."

"I can think of worse reasons for marrying people." He dumped the telephone on the bed. "And better ones."

Ellie dialed, and after a moment, said, "Hello? Oh, is this Mrs. Jenkins?" John Lamb began to laugh. "Could I speak to Mrs. Guardi, it's Miss Owen Spenser. Thank you." Then, covering the mouthpiece, "John, you're terrible!"

"Lulu Jenkins! I don't believe it."

"Mrs. Guardi? I have a friend staying with me who'd like to come over and take a few books from the library—would you mind?" Evidently, Mrs. Guardi would be delighted. "Thank you *so* much. He'll be over in a minute."

Two bulging semicircular bays rose the full three stories of the façade of Number 337, on each side of the front door. Like the door, each bay-window was topped with a profusion of carved horticulture; the left-hand bay was surmounted by a château-esque pointed spire, like a witch's hat, and the right-hand one—owing to some whim of the architect—by a different hat altogether: the one known in America as a "derby" and in England as a "bowler." Over the door, encircled by carved foliage, was the legend "Everywhere Be Bold" which the Spensers had adopted from the works of their supposed poet ancestor.

As before, the door was opened by the large and shapeless lady with the French accent. On this occasion she was attired in dark-green wool and a pale-yellow blouse; her hair, which was of the very light, rather sparse variety that is never tidy, was contained inside some kind of hairnet; by daylight, Lamb saw that she had a yellowish, somewhat blotchy skin, on which her features had been hastily assembled without regard for composition: eyes too far apart, nose too small, mouth too far from it, et cetera. John Lamb, who was not given to laughing at the old or the ugly, found her sad but not touching. Lulu Jenkins! That really was the final indignity!

She ushered him into a wide, dark hall, which some Spenser, at some time, had tried to make lighter and jollier by the application of a gaily flowered paper; for some reason which he did not have time to define, this had had the opposite effect. A rather magnificent curving staircase sprang up from the far end of the hall, lit by two arched windows—or rather, not lit by them, because they had been filled with stained glass in the most umbrageous Victorian colors which admitted no light at all. To left and right he glimpsed finely proportioned rooms, which, at a glance, he could tell had been decorated and furnished not in bad taste so much as in the wrong taste. As a decorator and furnisher of some talent and renown, he already knew that this was a house on which he would dearly love to get his itching hands. In the meantime, however, he had to turn his attention to the lady who was leasing it; she had come down the sweep of stairs and was advancing on him across the hall.

Mrs. Guardi's clothes and manner, not to mention the ring which flashed as she raised her hand to take his, told Lamb very clearly that this was a lady who could afford every penny of the "astronomical" rent which

Ellie's brother was charging her. Like many another well-heeled American woman he had met, it was difficult to tell her age, except that it was somewhere between forty-five and sixty; she carried her slim, not very tall body magnificently, and she offered her face to him (to any man, he was sure) in a manner which dared them not to take notice of the fact that she had once been a great beauty. She said, "Miss Owen Spenser said the 'library'; I think that must be the room upstairs which we call the study."

He noticed, as she turned to lead him back up the staircase, that her eyes were very dark, almost black; but this was not the only thing about them that struck him; they were curiously . . . he could think of no other word, matt. Matt and expressionless. With her dark hair—tinted possibly, but still her natural color he was inclined to think—and with her name, Guardi, he was perfectly prepared to believe that she was of Italian ancestry even if her voice was smoothly Boston. But the eyes were different. He had never met an Italian, even old, old ladies, whose eyes were not liquid and alive. There was no question of his being wise after the event; right from the start, Mrs. Amelia Guardi seemed to him to be a strange and interesting woman.

Perhaps it was for this reason that he became aware of the fact that even though the things they were saying to each other were the everyday unthinking politenesses, there was in her manner a kind of special awareness of him which he could not quite assess. After they had reached the wide hall at the top of the stairs, crossed it and moved into what she liked to call the study, he tested this suspicion by not answering one of her seemingly casual string of questions: How do you like San Francisco? Is this your first visit? Et cetera. "Oh," she had said, "just a vacation—that means you won't be staying long, what a pity!"

His silence, breaking the chain of social patter, stuck out like a drunk at a tea party. She turned and looked at him—and fell into his little trap by repeating it: "You probably won't be able to stay very long."

"A few weeks. Maybe a few months." It seemed to him that perhaps the edge of a smile touched her mouth; she knew that he knew that her questions were not merely casual; she knew that he had countered her with a purposely misleading answer, and it amused her. He found that he rather liked Mrs. Guardi. He said, "It's a very large house just for two women." After all, this was a game that could be played by more than one person.

"I like space. I'm writing a book, you know. Well . . ." She ended on an amused, and amusing, gesture of both hands, which added, "I naturally don't need to write for *money*." Naturally. It was his turn to smile. She waved an elegant, immaculately preserved hand at the room—at the arched bookshelves which lined the walls. "Take your pick. I hope you find what you want—they're a pretty dull lot."

"Thank you."

It caught his eye as he turned; indeed, how could it not catch his eye? It was standing on a desk near one of the windows. He must have given an involuntary gasp, because she noticed the direction of his glance and said, "That didn't come with the house, I assure you; I brought one or two of my own things."

He went to the desk so that he could look at it more closely—the Easter egg, clearly by Fabergé, resting in its golden stand on four beautifully fashioned clawlike legs: crimson enamel resplendent with rubies and pink pearls, pinpointed with diamonds, a magnificent piece.

Part II

THE
PSI

One

THREE MONTHS earlier, in that sour and shabby London bed-sittingroom, her eyes fixed on the dank November trees and the red Edwardian ugliness of Earl's Court outside the window, Mrs. Amelia Guardi had said, "I think you will do as I ask, if only because I'm a very rich woman."

When Mrs. Lulu Jenkins, as shabby and sour as the room, had said, "Money has nothing to do with it," she had, incredibly, meant every proud word. Just as the other woman had meant every word of her reply: "Money has something to do with everything."

Transferring her gaze to the ugly yellow bowl with the wizened orange and the two unripe bananas in it, and pulling her mink coat more closely about her slim dietary figure, Mrs. Guardi was wondering what the word "money" might conceivably mean to this messy, but unfortunately invaluable, ragbag of a woman. "When in doubt," her late husband had been fond of saying, "make an offer." Mrs. Guardi considered this advice carefully; though usually right, her late husband had, on one or two disastrous occasions, been very wrong indeed. While she considered, she continued to examine the Fabergé Easter egg, turning and turning it between slim, beautifully preserved hands so that Mrs. Jenkins might be able to appreciate it objectively—and the kind of "money" it represented. The rubies and diamonds flashed, even in this dim November light, but not more impressively than the rings on the fingers which held it; the pearls glowed richly, as did the magnificent double string encircling Mrs. Guardi's beautifully preserved neck, just visible between folds of mink.

Eventually, because she was a devious woman and because she knew something, though not much, about the shapeless female on the other side of the table, she made no further reference to financial transactions, but said, "Well . . . I'll be staying in London another three weeks—I want to be back in Connecticut for Christmas. I hope to be able to persuade you to change your mind before I leave."

The other woman, in that strange mixture of accents in which a French one undoubtedly predominated, said, "Please do not trouble yourself. I assure you I am perfectly decided."

"You see," the rich woman continued, ignoring her, "this matter is very near to my heart. I want the book, which I am going to write about it, to upset many scholars and many stupid preconceived notions . . ." She had not been mistaken; the other was too ingenuous, from the worldly point of view, to hide the sudden interest which had swept over her. Mrs. Guardi continued: "It's long past the time when such things should be treated scientifically—with respect, in the manner of any other scientific research; and I think that here"—she held up Monsieur Fabergé's glittering bauble— "is the chance of a lifetime." She glanced from under lowered lashes at the fat face confronting her. The eyes—such curious pale-green eyes—were

wide open, staring: not at the jeweled egg but at the
dream which the cleverer woman had implied that it
represented; the small lips—ridiculously small in such
a bag of a face—had unconsciously parted in greed: not
greed for money, but greed for a recognition long, long
(to the point of despair) denied. Mrs. Guardi decided
that the seed had been well and truly planted. Let it
germinate for a while undisturbed. She dropped the
whole subject abruptly, and said, almost roguishly,
"I've taken up enough of your valuable time, I can see
that, but you'll be hearing from me again, Mrs. Jenkins,
I don't give up at all easily."

Before the fat woman could think of any excuse for
prolonging the interview, before she could think of any
words which might hold the rich American for at least
a few minutes longer, Mrs. Amelia Guardi had slipped
the Easter egg back into its felt bag, and the bag had
disappeared into some inner recess of the sumptuous
coat as skillfully as Mrs. Guardi herself had disappeared from the room, leaving a faint whiff of Hermes
and a five-pound note lying on the table—double the
expected fee.

Lulu . . . Lou-lou . . . Louise Guichard had been
born and had lived until her twenty-fourth year in
Boulogne. Plump, moon-faced, she had dreamed away
her childhood in a good-natured daze, not caring
greatly that at school the other children laughed at her
and that she had no friends. For many years, too many
years, a placid good nature had been her most notice-
able attribute; well, in any case, it had *seemed* to be
placid good nature, whatever else it may really have
been somewhere deep inside the sturdy fortress of her

body. A dreamy girl, some people said—a deep one. Others were of the opinion that she was merely simple-minded. The truth lay uneasily between the two schools of thought.

Her parents, too busy running the small *épicerie* which was their livelihood, found her useless from the practical point of view, and from other points of view alarming. When the fishing boat *Marie Bellet*, in which her uncle worked, was missing for eleven long hours one foggy night, Louise had looked up from *Les Miserables*, through which she was at that time toiling, and had said, "He's dead—they're all dead." Eleven hours in fog was nothing; it could sometimes be bright and clear in midchannel, and then the boats would lie off until the fog cleared. However that might be, the wreckage of the *Marie Bellet* was found three days later; she had been run down by some larger vessel; none of the bodies ever reappeared. People could not have been said to like Louise very much more after this incident, but they began to entertain a grudging respect for her.

It was followed by others—concerning Madame Leforet's lost pearl brooch for instance, which Louise had said (without much interest, she didn't like Madame Leforet) would be found in the drain at the end of the rue Beauvais—concerning François Dubedan, reported killed in what was then known as Indo-China, but stated by Louise to be alive, though sick, and on his way home. He eventually turned up in a hospital in Paris suffering from loss of memory and identification tags, and was presently reunited with his family.

When questioned about these visitations of second sight, Louise would shrug and say that she "just

knew." Needless to say, various apocryphal examples
were added to the true ones, so that by the time she
reached her early twenties Louise Guichard was something of a character in that small area of Boulogne
where she happened to live.

In other communities, in other countries perhaps,
Louise might have been persuaded to capitalize on her
"gifts," whatever they were, but her parents were
staunchly and conservatively Catholic, as were the
majority of their neighbors. They not only feared their
daughter, but were inclined to see more of the devil
than of God in her; their parish priest, while more
intelligent and pantheistic, was aware of the fact that
although Louise might be gifted in some unusual
directions, she was a good deal less than gifted intellec-
tually; he was not sure that she was mentally equipped
to stand up to the strain which could be thrust upon her
if her capabilities were overexposed. Jolly Jackie Jenkins, however, suffered from no such qualms.

Nobody ever discovered what Jolly Jackie was doing
in Boulogne that autumn. Nobody even thought to ask
until he had lifted Louise from the bosom of her family,
whisked her off to London, and married her. Inquiries
would possibly have led to Skegness, an unsalubrious
seaside town on the drafty east coast of England,
where he had, that summer, been appearing in a revue
called *Girlie-Go-Round*. The police there were mildly
interested in him, though not interested enough to
follow him out of the county, let alone to France; but
Jackie Jenkins was nothing if not cautious.

Exactly how he first heard about Louise Guichard
and her mysterious "gifts" is also open to question, as
is the speed and efficiency with which he went about

wooing and winning her. Somewhere along the line she had undoubtedly flowered into womanhood; the process did not seem to have worried her, and it had certainly not worried any of the local boys; they were polite and civil to her, because the average Frenchman, whatever his social standing, is a polite and civil creature, but they had never looked upon her as desirable or even feminine, particularly as the family *épicerie* was dying on its feet, eaten away by the competition of the garish supermarket which had suddenly sprouted from the corner opposite it. Louise Guichard carried no dowry.

For Jolly Jackie, however, she carried something of infinitely greater price. He was a handsome, though fast-fading, man in his early forties; no one will ever know what he whispered to Louise in the shadows of the Citadel on those chill autumn nights, but in any case he was a past master of glib repartee, and the sexual angle would have worried him not at all; he had slept with all kinds of women for all kinds of purposes, and on the whole, he liked them large, big-breasted, and young. As for the face—as he had doubtless quipped in many a saloon bar—what difference did that make when the lights were out?

Once his hefty bride was safely married and in London—with a picture postcard of Trafalgar Square dispatched to her parents acquainting them of the fact, but giving no address—he felt secure to consider the future. (He had correctly assessed that his parents-in-law, whom he had met once, would simply be relieved to find themselves rid of their useless, dowryless, and large-appetited daughter.) His original intention had been to use his wife to bolster the shaky foundations of the conjuring act which he had been trailing around Great Britain, with diminishing success, for the past fifteen years. However, he very soon realized that though she could be made the basis of a stunning performance, there were other, more interesting ways of using her.

He borrowed some money, with difficulty, and leased a house in one of the more presentable streets in Chelsea, which at that time was very far from being the fashionable stomping ground for retarded adolescents of all ages which it has since become. He then, after some initial research, which paid off handsomely, let it be known in certain circles that there was this fabulous Frenchwoman in Chelsea whose powers were literally unlimited, "but, my dear, she's booked simply *months* ahead, it's impossible to get an appointment." During the months in question, by dint of living very frugally indeed off the loan, he managed to teach Louise a little English; he also found an "interpreter," a French-woman who had once been part of an adagio act with which he had shared a bill during his more palmy days. For the rest, he relied upon the fact that most of the proposed clients, which is to say, the class of client he intended to catch, would be able to speak a little French in varying degrees.

Because of this preparation, because Jolly Jackie was a better producer than he had ever been performer, and because of the extraordinary powers which Louise undoubtedly possessed, she very soon became an enormous success and it really did become impossible to get an appointment with her. Naturally, the fees rose as the demand rose, and before the end of the first year Mr. and Mrs. Jenkins were making more money than either of them would have believed possible. During the second year—and in spite of the lost weeks of profit—they even took a holiday at Cannes. In November of the third year (as a simple priest in Boulogne had once foreseen) the strain proved too much; the mysterious gift collapsed from overexposure, and no drug, no holiday, no doctor could entice it to return. For a further three months, to his wife's enormous but ignored distress, Jackie Jenkins managed to maintain the illusion—with declining success as he had maintained so many others. Only the reputation which Louise had so swiftly and surely earned made even this deception possible. In March of the fourth year Jolly Jackie disappeared, and all the money disappeared with him.

Abandoned like some gasping whale upon this foreign shore, Louise faced disaster, if not with equanimity, then with a return to the blank uncomplaining vegetable acceptance of her youth. If it had not been for the generosity of one of her old clients, with whose dead husband Louise had apparently established unusual rapport, she might possibly have starved to death. None of the symptoms from which she was suffering were quite applicable to ordinary people, but insofar as they were, the various doctors whose bills the grateful client uncomplainingly paid, came to the conclusion that Mrs. Jenkins was undergoing some kind of nervous breakdown. The grateful client sent Louise to a rest home in Surrey and paid her bills until, towards the end of the year, she departed to rejoin her husband.

By this time Louise had more or less recovered from what ailed her. For some reason which she did not bother to define (she seldom defined reasons), the last thing she considered doing was to return to Boulogne. She was now nearly twenty-eight, a large clumsy woman with washed-out pale-green eyes and an odd accent which was part French, part Jolly Jackie's native cockney, and part something more classy which he had endeavored to teach her in order to impress the customers. She never even thought about the powers she had once possessed, but worked at the most humble jobs she could find: cleaning (not very thorough), washing up (too clumsy), taking in sewing (too myopic).

It could not be said that she actually made any friends, she still had no aptitude for that; but oddly enough, it was through the determination of something like a friend—a small, mousy woman who lived in the room across the hall from her, that she eventually drifted back into the only occupation for which she had any talent at all. Cajoled into reading Miss Oliphant's palm—an occupation for which Louise had nothing but contempt—she realized that the power, whatever it was, had at last returned to her, unbidden as ever. Without thinking, and certainly without recourse to any of the lines which time had etched on Miss Oliphant's worn little hand, Louise recounted to that startled person many events of her youth which Miss Oliphant herself had all but forgotten.

And so, once again—but timidly, nursing whatever of the old strength she once again possessed (or which possessed her, however it might be)—she dealt with any clients that Miss Oliphant, or fate, brought her way. In a tiny, barely noticed echo of the éclat, which had once been hers so briefly, she even began to make a reputation: "My dear, there's this extraordinary woman living in Earl's Court . . ." It was not much of a reputation, because Louise herself (or Lulu, as she had somehow come to be called along the way) was not very interested in it; like many another true artist, she knew with certainty that she was capable of great things; the power she had possessed, and seemed to possess again, was a true power; if fate had decreed that it was never to be used to its full extent, so be it; like many another true artist, she was unable to come to terms with the world of realities—she didn't speak its language and it didn't speak hers. She was forty, and looked anything from five to ten years older; the next thing of any interest at all that was likely to happen to her was death—coming early, in all probability, because she was incapable of looking after herself properly—and even death would be of questionable interest to her, since she'd be dead, and of no interest whatever to anyone else. Except . . .

Except for the fact that three or four of the people who had "discovered" her, in this later phase of her life, were fanatical in their praise of her—and one of them, reasonably rich but mean, who liked Lulu because she was cheap, happened to meet Mrs. Amelia Guardi at a cocktail party.

Amelia Guardi realized almost immediately that Lulu was what she had been searching for during the three years since her husband's death. As might have been expected, because her ordinary intelligence was extremely limited, it took Lulu Jenkins a great deal longer to realize that Mrs. Guardi was what *she* had been searching for; it also took a certain amount of guile on the part of the rich American, because, in fact, Lulu had not been searching for anything in particular; she had merely stumbled over her destiny yet again. Since the first stumble had landed her in the arms of Jolly Jackie Jenkins, it was probably just as well that she was incapable of equating cause with effect.

Their next meeting, which was to affect so many other lives apart from their own, took place in Mrs. Guardi's suite at Claridge's. There was a subtle design in this, as in most other things that the rich American woman planned. In the first place, the room in Earl's Court had disgusted her, and she saw no reason to upset herself over such negligible details; more important, she knew that she would break something of this fat white spider's power once she had removed it from the shadowy corner where it had built its web—for Mrs. Guardi, unlike almost every other person who had ever dealt with Lulu Jenkins, was very much aware of this power; she never made the mistake of patronizing the lumpy woman whose patroness she intended to be. Lulu was not intelligent, as the ratings of this generally rather unintelligent world go, but who could tell by what other, and swifter, means she might arrive at correct conclusions? Mrs. Guardi, more intelligent than most, certainly could not.

Mrs. Jenkins had put on her best dress, her best coat, hat and shoes. Though bizarre, the effect was a considerable improvement on the grubby garment of dark-pink flannel which she had worn in Earl's Court. Tea—a carefully ordered affair which went a long way beyond the kind of thing Claridge's usually had to offer—was served with ceremony; there was a profusion of the kind of cakes which Mrs. Guardi had surmised, correctly, that her guest would most enjoy. During this sumptuous but schoolgirlish repast, Mrs. Guardi was careful not to discuss the matter in hand, but she managed to make references to the president of The British Society for Psychical Research, with whom she had lunched the day before, the publishers, both in London and New York, who had already shown interest in her proposed book, and the name of the eminence of eminents who was prepared to write its introduction. Lulu Jenkins absorbed every word like some giant sponge, just as, like some giant child, she devoured her way through hot buttered toast, scones, cucumber sandwiches, and a variety of cakes.

When all this was over, Amelia Guardi said, "Now, I *do* hope I'm going to be able to persuade you to help me in this very important task—not just for yourself, Lulu"—she really must learn not to shudder, even inwardly, when she pronounced that name— "but for science, for posterity."

"Would I . . . Would I be . . . mentioned in the book?"

At this question, so long expected but so much more ingenuous in form than was ever expected, Amelia Guardi gave her artificial but nonetheless charming little laugh: "*Mentioned!* Why Lulu, what do you take me for? We shall be co-authors; in fact, I have never since I met you thought of my name in anything but second place. I have many faults, my dear, but I am not selfish and not vain."

The pale-green, myopic eyes were as bright now as she had ever seen them; the small mouth had fallen open again; somewhere in that extraordinary being the days of success and admiration, under the aegis of

Jackie Jenkins, had left an indelible mark; to this extent
at least Lulu was totally human. Now, far away at the
end of the long dark tunnel of years since he had
abandoned her, she saw another glow of glory coming
nearer—a day when the name of Louise Jenkins would
be on every mouth—a day when her great gift would
be generally acknowledged. "My dear, have you
read . . . ? My dear, you simply *must* read . . ."

Mrs. Guardi had considered the figures involved very
carefully; as far as this poverty-stricken creature was
concerned, whatever she offered would seem immense;
it was true that at some time in the past she had
apparently earned good money, but it was doubtful if
the disgraceful character she called husband had ever
allowed her to know exactly how much. Mrs. Guardi
could afford to give away a great deal of money
without noticing it, but she knew that to certain minds
large sums are always suspect. Therefore, in her most
practical tone of voice, she named the conservative but
not ungenerous figures she had finally decided upon: "I
will pay all your expenses, of course. On top of this I'd
like you to take five hundred dollars a week for a
guaranteed period of six months. That makes a total of
thirteen thousand dollars—or, if you like, something
like five thousand four hundred pounds sterling, or a
little over sixty thousand francs . . ."

She could see that the other woman's mind was
already reeling about, drunk with these figures, so she
finished quickly: "The guarantee means that if our
work only took four months, or four weeks, you would
still receive this sum; and of course, it would only be
fair to make an advance of two thousand dollars now, if
you agree." This last would, she hoped, enable Mrs.

Jenkins to buy some other clothes before they were, inevitably, seen in public together.

"Since the average person is incurably small-minded and curious, it would obviously be to our advantage if we called you . . . Let's see—my 'secretary-companion' why not?"

And so the extraordinary pact was sealed, meaning such different things to each of them. Later, after they had drunk to success with a little sherry, Lulu had gazed for a time in bemused silence at the woman who was now her employer, and had eventually said, "I don't see when . . . I mean, where . . . I don't see how we shall begin our . . . work."

"That's my problem, my dear. You mustn't worry your head about such things." It was not a very satisfactory answer, and the woman who gave it would certainly not have been satisfied with it. Lulu Jenkins merely nodded vaguely; generally speaking, the less she was asked to worry her head about anything, the happier she was; therefore, to an extent, the answer made her happy, but on the other hand, it seemed to have uneasy overtones which she was not able to pin down; much of her life was spent in this state of semi-awareness because her memory, in the ordinary everyday sense of the word, was so bad; she might or might not come to remember that the two sentences, "That's my problem, my dear. You mustn't worry your head about such things," had been much used by her long-vanished husband.

She was jerked out of her ruminations by the presence of the Fabergé Easter egg; although she was, in fact, looking at it, vision recorded an impression long after some other, deeper sense. Amelia Guardi noticed the instinctive reaction and was pleased by it; she now held the egg out over the remains of Lulu's gargantuan tea and said, "Yes, I know it alarms you, but I wanted to make a note of that room you described the other day, do you remember?"

Lulu rarely remembered what she actually said when the power was moving in her, though occasionally it came back to her when another person or another incident reminded her, but only half remembered, and often attended by some attached and often frightening emotion, fear or jealousy or a pang of utter loss. Her worlds did not live easily together. She therefore took the bejeweled egg with some distaste, because she knew that the things associated with it were not pleasant. Encouragingly, Mrs. Guardi said, "It was so vivid. I should have made a note at the time, but I wasn't prepared."

Lulu could make no sense whatever of all this talk about notes, but the formless chippolata-fingers had already closed around the egg, and the glittering object seemed almost to vibrate within them as if, through their prescience, it was generating some energy of its own.

The fat woman said, "The time . . . The room . . . I don't think . . ." But then her voice tailed away. She turned her head slightly, gazing at the silver-plated hotel teapot. The pale-green eyes, fixed on one glittering silver highlight, seemed to grow yet paler, as though they would eventually fade away altogether, becoming white.

After a time she sighed deeply. "Such unhappiness!" There was another long silence; then: "Cypresses. Five tall cypresses in a line." London's traffic growled and bellowed in some other cycle of time. Amelia Guardi sat very still, watching this unappetizing but infinitely precious lump of woman with all the considerable concentration of which she was capable.

"Sunlight. The . . . The sea. No, perhaps a lake. Five tall cypresses." She shook her massive head and sighed again, a sigh of infinite sadness. "Such unhappiness— such tears!" The pale eyes did not waver from the gleam of light on the teapot. "The room . . ." She shuddered. "A red room."

Mrs. Guardi leaned forward a little.

"Yes, a bedroom. The bed in the center under an . . . an arch. Tears, always tears." Another great sigh made her big body shake. "*Three* arches. The bed in the middle. The others . . . Yes, the others are windows." She frowned. There was a cacophony of blowing horns and explicit London dialogue in the street outside where the twentieth century was showing signs of bursting at the seams, but they did not affect Lulu Jenkins, who was in another place. "At the top of each arch . . . a face. Man and goat. And flowers. Falling flowers. The room . . ." Again the frown. "Yes, it's a round room." Again for a long time she was silent, odd shadows of thoughts and emotions which may or may not have been her own flitting across the massive face, so unresponsive in real life, so infinitely sensitive in other spheres. "Always this unhappiness . . . Sunlight . . . cypresses . . . Half-man, half-goat." She shuddered. Mrs. Guardi was astonished to see that the fat cheeks were wet with tears.

After a moment, with a visible effort, Lulu Jenkins wrenched her eyes away from the teapot and looked vaguely at the glittering piece of Fabergé, as if surprised to find it in her hands. She placed it on the tea tray, next to a demolished walnut cake.

Mrs. Guardi smiled. "Remarkable! Quite remarkable!"

Lulu, having returned to daily life, was now her old self, bemused. "A *red* bedroom!" She clearly disapproved. "And round!" Dim images of a time long ago stirred in her mind—a holiday by a blue sea where there had been cypresses. "It seemed . . . Southern. Warm. I was once in Cannes."

Amelia Guardi picked up the egg and held it up to the light. The enamel gleamed like fresh blood. All she said was, "We shall see."

Lulu had no idea what that was supposed to mean. "We shall see." *What* would she see?

What she saw—six weeks later when Richard Owen Spenser opened a door, saying, "I guess you could call this the principal bedroom"—was a round room with three arches facing the door. In the central arch, recessed, was a big bed, and in the other two were tall windows. The top of each arch was decorated with carved swags of flowers, falling, and at the center of each swag was a carved face, half-man, half-goat—the face of a grinning satyr.

Lulu Jenkins let out a gasp and fell back against the doorpost, causing the whole room, if not the whole house, to shudder. Mrs. Guardi's pleasure at her surprise was marred by the terrible thought that she might be upon the brink of a heart attack. From the expression on young Richard's face, he was thinking the same thing.

"My companion," said Amelia Guardi hastily, "is rather tired; she isn't used to travel, you see."

Lulu was seated—not in the bedroom, she wouldn't have that—and brought cups of tea. Later, when the young man had gone, leaving them in possession of this vast place, which Lulu could still not believe her employer had actually rented, she was inclined to be tearful. "The shock! I'm not as strong as I look, Mrs. Guardi—we naturals are very, very sensitive, you know."

Amelia Guardi, who was getting to know this familiar fairly well by now, was murmurously solicitous; she knew that the recriminations would be short-lived because a more natural native curiosity was longing to be let out.

After a time: "But how . . . how did you find it? How *could* you have found it?"

"From your description, Lulu."

The washed-out green eyes stared in astonishment across the chasm of differences which separated them. The power of Lulu's very special gifts barely astonished Mrs. Guardi more than the power of Mrs. Guardi's money astonished Lulu. "But I . . . hardly described anything."

"The room. That was enough." She drew up a chair and sat down. "Together with the Fabergé Easter egg, it was enough. You see, Lulu, there are only a certain number of pieces of genuine Fabergé in the world. The finest ones—and this is very fine—are all listed, all have a pedigree. The ruby egg was given by the Czarina to Queen Alexandra, and *she* gave it to one of her ladies-in-waiting. When the family fell on hard times, in the twenties, it was sold. You see?"

Lulu saw that for a woman like Mrs. Guardi, all kinds of quite impossible things were perfectly possible; there had even been a beautiful young man with a beautiful car waiting for them at San Francisco airport.

"Since then, it has had four owners, including my late husband. The first one lived in London; he was very rich, and had some kind of fixation about being robbed, so he kept his whole collection in the bank, which can't have given him very much pleasure. Anyway, I knew we wouldn't find cypresses and a blue sea there. The second lived in New York, and he had at one time owned a villa at Cap d'Antibes. But the people who went to look at it on my behalf . . ."

"What people?"

"Private detectives, Lulu."

"!"

"They assured me that there was no room in that villa at all like the one you'd described—nor at his house on Long Island. I didn't think there would be, not on Long Island, but it was worth checking. This man lost most of his money in the Depression; he had to sell his Fabergés.

"That left the third owners, the ones who had owned it before my husband. They had lived in San Francisco, so the Inquiry Agency sent a man to look at their house—this house. And in this house he found . . ." She gestured in the direction of the circular bedroom with the three arches. *"Voilà!"*

"And the cypresses?"

Mrs. Guardi urged her to get to her feet; then led her out of the small book-lined room in which they had been sitting, across the upstairs hall, and into the circular bedroom. Lulu Jenkins paused just inside the door, staring suspiciously at the unobtrusive golden wallpaper. "Red walls," she said. "Surely I said red walls?"

"Silk—red Chinese silk, but it wore out. However, several people apparently remembered it from the old days."

Lulu nodded. Mrs. Guardi beckoned from the window where she was standing, and the other woman thudded across the room to join her. Below them was a leafy, somewhat overgrown garden which plunged in awkward terraces down the hillside towards the roof of the neighboring house, over which could be seen the marina and the Bay. Edging the second terrace stood a row of five tall cypresses. Lulu nodded again; then turned and looked back at the room behind them. She was evidently listening very intently. Amelia Guardi also listened; she heard a car passing in the street, a child laughing far away, the whine of jet engines somewhere high overhead. She wondered what it was that Lulu Jenkins heard. The big woman surprised her by saying suddenly, without turning, "Who is that in the garden?"

A *frisson* of fear running lightly up her spine, Mrs. Guardi turned towards the window. There was nobody in the garden. Lulu said, "A girl in a blue dress, picking roses."

She did not seem to be surprised to be told that the girl was not there; she merely nodded to herself, coming to some unguessable conclusion of her own. "Yes," she said. "This is the place."

Three weeks later, a few days after Ellie had returned from Europe, Mrs. Guardi looked out of her bedroom window one morning and saw her in the garden; she was wearing a blue dress and picking roses.

Two

THE PRESENCE of Amelia Guardi and Lulu Jenkins, that oddly assorted pair, at Number 337 did not cause much comment in Gilman Street. Several of the big old mansions had long ago been turned into expensive apartment houses, and the presence of strangers, even—alas—transients, though a regrettable occurrence in the opinion of "the right people" did not cause the kind of furor it would have caused in an earlier day. Of course, Mrs. Guardi, seen occasionally stepping from the front door to the door of a chauffeur-driven limousine, was immediately recognized as being "a right person."

These excursions were apparently devoted to what she called her "research"—a word which meant nothing to Lulu, who never set foot outside the house. The fact that she was visiting, for the first and probably the last time in her life, one of the world's fascinating cities meant, it would seem, nothing to her; the view from various windows sufficed. But then, it is a mistake to judge a woman like Lulu Jenkins by the standards of other people; possibly, from her chair in a darkened room, she knew more of the city in more of its aspects, past and present, than all its other inhabitants put together.

The only times the two women ever entered each

other's orbit were for meals and—the raison d'être of their existence—those long evening sessions of "work."

Grace and Teresa, the black ladies who came every day to cook and clean, respectively, seemed to find nothing odd about the life that went on in the big house; perhaps they had long ago decided that everything about Pacific Heights was odd anyway; they spent their time in complicated and sometimes passionate discussion concerning the vagaries of their husbands and children; since they were both equipped with magnificent voices, this endless confabulation was able to continue however many rooms separated them. As far as Mrs. Guardi was concerned, they could do as they liked, for not only did they mind their own business with ferocity, but Grace was a superb cook and Teresa kept the few rooms which they were using in spotless condition.

It was just as well that patience and self-control were two attributes with which Amelia Guardi had armed herself over the years. (She had not been born with them.) When it came to the business of explaining to Lulu the exact purpose of their presence in San Francisco and at Number 337, she had to contend not only with the big woman's inability to link cause and effect, but with something deeper and more mutinous which she herself was unable to understand very clearly, and which Lulu would not, or more possibly could not, elucidate. In time—and time in this case meant a matter of wearying weeks—the latter gradually revealed itself as something like fear. Lulu was afraid of the house and of what it had once contained—and for her, still did contain. Their purpose in renting the place, which seemed to Mrs. Guardi very simple, had to be repeated many times, in whole or in part, with great stress laid on the hoped-for results, and the publicity and fame which they must certainly bring.

While these explanations were in progress, Lulu would sit, slumped in her favorite chair like a sack of apples, occasionally darting pale-green glances at the explainer, and even more occasionally asking questions, many of which demonstrated quite clearly that her attention had wandered away in time or space and that this particular repetition was not going to be the last. Whether or not Amelia Guardi banged her head against the wall in the privacy of her own rooms, she never for one moment allowed any note of irritation to color her voice as she talked, and talked, and talked to Lulu. If she felt like a desert traveler whose single camel has settled down to rest forever a hundred miles from the nearest water, she never showed it. But then, she was a remarkable woman.

Prior to her meeting with Lulu, she had visited many mediums, finding most of them false and the others only weakly endowed. Three of them, however, when the Fabergé egg was placed in their hands had recoiled and had mentioned blood. Did Lulu understand thus far. Lulu would dart a pale-green glance, sniff and nod.

Now then, unlike many famous pieces of Fabergé, the ruby, diamond, and pearl egg had not been inundated by the Revolution, with all its attendant horrors. No—its well-attested history was calm and mild. It had left the Czarina's hands many years before the final horrors of Ekaterinberg, and though the Queen of England to whom she had given it had not led a very happy life, married to that tiresome husband, she had, historically, not taken a knife to him—as many another woman might have done. Her lady-in-waiting's family had simply grown poor gently, and had parted with the egg, among many other possessions far more valuable, without bloodletting of any kind. The wealthy Englishman who had bought it had died in his bed at the age of eighty-six, perfectly sure that there were burglars in the next room, but otherwise in peace, since all his valuables were in a vault in the City. The New Yorker who had subsequently bought it had admittedly been forced to sell it by the Depression, but as far as he was concerned, disaster had been short-lived, and he had quite quickly made another fortune, married three more wives, and lived to a ripe old age before dropping dead quite suddenly while opening a bottle of bourbon with an anticipatory smile on his lips.

That left Mrs. Guardi's own husband—a Fabergé collector of unblemished reputation as far as blood was concerned, allowing for the fact that he occasionally donated it—and the Spensers.

The Spensers. They had owned the Fabergé egg; they had built this house and lived in it—and no one but a Spenser had lived in it until Mrs. Guardi herself had rented it last month. Hadn't Lulu herself, on that first day here, said, "Yes, this is the place"? Indeed she had. Was Lulu following?

Several times Lulu had proved that far from following, she was on another road in another part of the forest, going in the opposite direction. But finally, grudgingly, she had admitted that the Spensers, the Fabergé Easter egg, her own (and others') sense of blood—all these intersected neatly in one place: Number 337 Gilman Street, San Francisco.

So now, persisted Mrs. Guardi with infinite and unabated patience, what about the Spensers themselves? They were an odd family, as any old local gossip would very soon attest. There were secrets. For instance, nobody knew what violent disagreement had parted forever the two brothers, Harold and Owen—a disagreement so violent that it had caused Owen to pack up, lock, stock, and barrel, and take his entire family across the continent to Philadelphia, never speaking to his brother again. There were secrets, but if blood had been spilled in violence, nobody knew about it. Didn't Lulu see what that meant? No, Lulu did not see—would not see for a long time—what that meant.

It meant that here in this house lay the perfect subject for research—for true psychic research. For here in this house there had been unhappiness and violence and the spilling of blood—that much they already knew for certain. Now they were going to work together, and they were going to discover, by psychic means (for there were no others available to them), exactly how and when and where these things had occurred. Didn't Lulu *see*?

At last, at long last, a faint glimmering behind the uncanny eyes, a faint movement of the body showed that Lulu could perceive a ray of reason, and was excited by it.

Having discovered the truth, what were they going to do? They were going to *publish* the truth, yes. Think of the furor, the shock, even the mockery, for what did mockery matter when they knew that they were right

—when they knew that in the end their work would force the mundane world into making its own mundane inquiries, and that those inquiries must inevitably lead to a like truth—because truth *will* out, and nothing on God's earth can stop it. Didn't Lulu *see*?

At last Lulu's eyes were on fire with a vision of glory. Yes, of course, it was true; never before had purely psychic research revealed facts hitherto unknown. It would be the breakthrough . . .

"It will be the breakthrough," cried Mrs. Guardi for the fifth or sixth time. "Faced with evidence like that, even the most critical will have to admit the existence of another dimension. It's my greatest ambition, Lulu, my only ambition—it always has been. And never, never has this poor sick world needed a spiritual affirmation as it needs one now."

Glory shone from the eyes of Lulu Jenkins, the Great Lulu Jenkins. Vindication. Triumph. Acclaim. Moreover, somewhere, in some inevitable slough of despond, Jolly Jackie would hear the echoes of it and know the true value of what he had so lightly and so callously cast away.

Hoping that she wasn't piling it on a little too thickly, Amelia Guardi added, "And it will all be your doing, Lulu. Your name will be a household word." She saw that at least one thing was certain—she would not have to explain it ever again. The whole shapeless mass of the other woman was quivering with excitement. At last. It had taken many weeks.

In order to give the vision time for a full flowering, she turned away to occupy herself with the preparations of their usual evening session, placing the tape recorder in position (Lulu didn't like the tape recorder,

but it was a necessity), and then selecting an unused
tape from the shelf where they were neatly stacked.
After this she placed a silver candlestick, holding a tall
yellow candle, on the table in front of Lulu, who was
still wrapped in dreams of glory; she lit the candle
carefully, coaxing the wick so that the flame burned
straight and true. Then she drew the curtains across
the four tall windows, making sure there were no
chinks, before coming back to the table, where she
stood staring for a time, thoughtfully, at Mrs. Jenkins,
whose sausage-fingers were playing with the long rope
of amber beads she liked to wear looped twice around
the place where her head joined her body—it could
hardly have been called a neck. Since the spell had to
be broken some time, she said, very softly, "Lulu?"

Mrs. Jenkins came slowly and unwillingly out of her
delicious reverie. Amelia Guardi took her place on the
other side of the table; she removed the Fabergé egg
from its velvet bag and placed it near the candle. Lulu
looked at it with distaste. Mrs. Guardi opened a black
notebook and studied it for a time in silence; then, "It's
fascinating," she said, "how the names are all beginning to fit.

"Names?"

Mrs. Guardi sighed inwardly, at the same time
smiling across the table. "Would you like me to play
back the last tape?"

Lulu shook her head, turning that baleful gaze from
the egg, glittering toy of an old era, to the recorder,
glittering toy of a new one. She could not have said
which of them made her the more uncomfortable.

"Well," said Mrs. Guardi, experienced by now and
therefore undaunted, "let's just see where we stand.

Last night it became quite obvious that the source of all this unhappiness which you mentioned in London is Stella; that's the last Mrs. Spenser, Mrs. Harold Spenser."

"Always crying."

"It seems she had good reason. Her husband committed suicide."

"Not here, not in this house."

Amelia Guardi gave her a quick look of genuine surprise and admiration; these two emotions were quite often mixed with the habitual oil of flattery with which she kept their relationship in smooth running order. "You really are an astonishing person, Lulu."

"There are things I just know."

"You're right. I was down at the library this afternoon reading old newspapers; they keep them all on microfilm, you know."

"!"

"It happened in 1928. He took his car and drove south down the coast; they found him on some beach; he'd shot himself. Perhaps that's why you never mention him."

Gazing into the candle flame, Lulu said, "But there is a man. He's . . . close now."

The look which Amelia Guardi now gave her was a much sharper one. "The one Stella keeps calling? Michael—Mikey?"

Lulu nodded. The candle flame suddenly flickered wildly, as if in a draft—but there was no draft in the closely curtained and locked room. Mrs. Guardi's hands gripped the edge of the table; then, relaxing, fell back to her lap. The candle flame was still again.

"He was her second husband. I was reading the

reports of the wedding; she met him . . . some years after Harold's death."

"Crying, always crying." Lulu's voice had slurred; she was staring intently at the flame.

"He was a whole lot younger than she was."

"Many women."

"What?"

Lulu did not answer. She had sagged lower in the heavy chair. Mrs. Guardi said, "You see, we're getting near the date of . . . of whatever happened here. She didn't marry this Michael—Michael Burke until 1936; by that time the little boy, Patrick, was dead . . . ."

"Piggy."

"Yes. I think that must have been a nickname. There seem to have been three other children—Hugh, Leona and Catherine. I think they must be dead by now too, or the house wouldn't have passed to the other branch of the family."

Lulu suddenly said, in a voice which was and was not her own, "Piggy wants to play jigsaws."

Amelia Guardi knew that soon it would begin. She leaned forward, speaking very distinctly. "Lulu, this Michael—is he here?"

"Close. All close. Very . . . strong tonight."

"I think we must try to reach him. We must try to reach Michael. I've a feeling that he's at the center of it all—all the weeping, all the unhappiness, and perhaps . . . perhaps the blood, too. Lulu?"

"Crying, always crying."

"Lulu, I'm going to try to guide you tonight."

"*They* guide me."

"But there are things we *must* know. For our research—for our book."

Even the magic words "our book" could not reach Lulu Jenkins now. Mrs. Guardi pushed the Fabergé Easter egg towards her; the rubies and diamonds caught fire from the candle, winking and glittering; the pink pearls exuded their mysterious inner light, needing no other. Lulu touched it with one ungainly hand, and a shudder made her massive body quake like some collapsed, ill-set blancmange. Mrs. Guardi pressed the start-button of the tape recorder and sat back in her chair.

The flame of the candle was reflected in each wide-open unblinking green eye. The breathing had become slower, heavier. The two fat hands made a soft nest, in which the egg lay inert, full of secrets.

Again the candle flame flickered as if somebody had passed swiftly near to the table. Mrs. Guardi watched, tense, holding her breath, appalled, even though it was something she had watched every night for weeks now. The pale-green eyes rolled slowly upwards, slowly, slowly, until the pouchy upper lids hid them completely, and only the white sightless eyeballs were left to catch the reflection of the no-longer-troubled candle.

The form it took was never the same twice; it always surprised, and sometimes horrified, her. This time the big, shapeless face began to grimace, eyebrows and mouth working in some kind of agitation. For a moment, ridiculously, Mrs. Guardi found herself looking at a fat woman asleep on a summer's afternoon, being bothered by a fly. Then, sharply, making her start, a sharp, thin voice, quite unlike Lulu's snapped, "Who's there? Who *is* that out there?" A tense, listening pause; then: "Catherine, is that you? For Christ's sake, go

away, get out of here! Always poking and prying . . .
Catherine?"

Silence. Again the fat face began to work with
agitated emotion, which formed itself gradually into
sobs—a rising crescendo of sobs. The voice emerged,
strangled by misery: "Oh God, oh dear God, what can I
do? I didn't mean it—Mikey, I didn't mean it. Come
back, my darling, come back, Mikey, *please* come
back!" The voice was overwhelmed by another fit of
weeping—the racking sobs of utterly abandoned grief;
but the fat bulk of the woman who was emitting them
remained motionless. Like the neat machine on the
table, only its two spools turning, Lulu Jenkins herself
was a recorder.

After a long time the paroxysm passed away—
slowly and painfully. And there was dead silence.

Mrs. Guardi was used to these pauses now. Shadows
of thought and emotions belonging to people long dead
flitted about the massive, collapsed face on the other
side of the table. This pause lasted exactly seven and a
half minutes by Mrs. Guardi's elegant watch. During
it—in two quite different voices—Lulu said, "I *don't*
want to go to dancing class," and, "Piggy wants to play
Snakes and Ladders." Once, laughter emerged: stupid,
giggling laughter. And then, again, quite suddenly, the
features twisted themselves into a terrifying mask of
rage, and the voice burst out of the flaccid lips in a
torrent of venom which they would have been quite
incapable of producing in real life: "Get away from me!
Don't touch me, don't come near me!" Then rapid,
furious breathing. Then: "I don't want to hear your lies,
I'm sick to death of your lies. I know where you've

been—you stink of it, you reek of it, you haven't even bothered to wash that damned cock you're so proud of. *Get away from me!*"

Amelia Guardi said, "Oh my God!" It might have meant anything—seemed to have been torn out of her by instinct. Once again the elegantly preserved hands were gripping the edge of the table; the black eyes were fixed on the writhing face opposite her.

"Get out of my room and take your fucking bribery with you." And, abruptly, taking Mrs. Guardi by surprise, the fat hands flung the Fabergé Easter egg violently away from them. She caught it at the very edge of the table and pushed it out of reach beyond the tape recorder.

The voice which was not that of Lulu Jenkins was now screaming, "I don't *want* a doctor, I won't *see* a doctor! Go away, go away, all of you!" Another storm of sobbing, this one dying away more quickly. Again silence.

Slowly, Amelia Guardi managed to make her body relax. After a moment she leaned across towards the inert bag of a body slumped low in the heavy chair and said, quietly but firmly, "Is Michael there?"

There was no response.

"We need to speak to Michael. Michael Burke. Mikey."

Lulu Jenkins emitted a low moan; she began to breathe deeply and with difficulty—agonized shudders of breath. Then she said, "No, no! Keep away from me! I can't stand blood, I can't *stand* it. For Christ's sake, *it's all over your hands!*" And, with a savage speed it would never have managed in real life, one plump hand shot forward from the inert body and slammed down onto the table, while the voice, as suddenly shrill with terror, shouted, "*No!* Don't touch that *knife!*"

Ellie's cry made John Lamb swing around in fear. He saw the knife spin away from her fingers—from the block on which she had been slicing onions—and clatter onto the tiled floor, where it lay, spinning. Ellie herself stood very still, staring at it, one hand pressed to her mouth so that he thought she must have cut herself. He went to her quickly and put an arm around her. "What happened?"

Ellie removed the hand from her mouth, revealing that there was no blood on it; she raised her head from that scrutiny of the knife, which had now spun itself to a standstill, and looked at him blankly.

"Ellie, what *happened?*" It was the blankness in her, these last few days, which scared him as much as anything.

"Nothing. I just . . . dropped it."

"You let out a yell that must have curdled the milk."

"I did?" He could see her struggling to think of some justification for the yell which she was clearly unaware of having emitted; he was used to the justifications too; they scared him only a little less than the blankness.

"I guess I . . . I must have thought I'd cut myself."

Anxiety and fear wheeled over him, like a couple of vultures which had scented death, their shadows criss-crossing his path. Her movements, which had always been so sure and incisive, had become clumsy (witness the knife), and apathy enfolded her quick mind, so that answers were delayed, sometimes indefinitely. Dr. Hillier had breezily commanded rest, and so, daylong, she rested, sometimes pretending to read, until the book would sag onto her lap and she would be left staring into space. Once or twice he had even glimpsed odd changes of expression on her face during these periods of staring, as if she were listening to a conversation which he could not hear. At this point he had really been forced to take a grip on himself: after all, everybody's expression was apt to change in tune with their thoughts. Then what *were* these thoughts which absorbed her? She would not, or could not, say.

Hillier himself was not much help; he had apparently consulted "other opinions," tactfully, as promised; they had only served to corroborate his own: she had undergone a violent traumatic (useful word) psychosomatic (useful word) experience which had used up vast amounts of energy; this energy had now to be recouped; she was, in fact, convalescent. As for her outburst about family insanity, wasn't that a typical result of emotional overstrain? And, though Dr. Hillier didn't want to emphasize the fact, this whole thing *had* been brought about by the sexual act; wasn't it natural that there should be a concomitant emotional reaction against sex, i.e., marriage, and an irrational emotional excuse, insanity, to go with it.

John Lamb was neither convinced nor satisfied. There seemed to him to be something too pat—too conveniently prevaricating—about these opinions. Time would tell, Dr. Hillier seemed to be saying, thus excusing himself from having to make a definite statement one way or the other. Lamb also suspected that the man was finding it difficult to give him a direct and honest look in the eye.

His own attitude to what Ellie had told him remained ambivalent. Had she really played out that grotesque and sickening scene with Stefan in this very room? Or could it by chance have been another, earlier, attack of whatever had seized her while he himself had been making love to her on that disastrous night? Some imaginary sexual encounter had quite obviously been going on in her mind then, so it was surely possible that the seduction of the Yugoslav had been imaginary as well.

She had made him promise not to discuss any of it with Richie, but he knew that if she showed no sign of getting better, this was one promise which he was certainly going to break. ("Your girlfriend, Mr. Lamb," Richie had said at their first fogbound meeting, "is screwing my boyfriend—how does that grab you?" Yes, it was something they were going to have to discuss sooner or later.)

As for his research into her family, the books which he had taken from the big house had turned out to be useless and therefore frustrating. There were four of them. Unused to research, he found it incredible that so many hundreds of pages could promise so much and deliver so little; all four were remorselessly trivial and weighted down with awe. The first, published in 1920, consisted entirely of tea-party chatter printed and bound; the second (1934) was also compiled, rather than written, by a woman, and read like a first primer for anyone with the money and the inclination who sought to ascend the apparently slippery ladder of San Francisco "society." It gave little hope of success for the aspirant.

The third, *The Spensers of San Francisco* (1927), seemed initially to be what he was looking for, but after reading a hundred pages which did little more than list births, marriages, garden parties, christenings, balls, deaths, and successful investments, he recalled a page which he had noticed but skipped somewhere between the Foreword and the Introduction. (It was that kind of book.) This page was headed Acknowledgments, and explained the whole thing: *The Spensers of San Francisco* had been commissioned and paid for by the Spensers themselves. He put the book aside and picked up the final one.

This was called *City of Rogues.* The author, it appeared, came from the East and was not unduly impressed by any Western social pretensions; he started out with great panache, obviously intending to show how San Francisco had been founded, built up, and subsequently ruled sub rosa by twenty or so families no better than anyone else's and frequently a great deal worse. The early chapters, dealing with those "characters" who had long since become part of the city's brawny legend were thoroughly entertaining; they presented the men in question, Ellie's great-great-grandfather included, with most of their blemishes— among which, in Old Dick Spenser's case, insanity certainly didn't figure; but as the generations plodded towards the present, the long shadows of Burlingame and Pacific Heights had fallen across the pages, scaring the poor author and his publisher out of their wits, so that the whole project collapsed in a snobbish mire of dull ambiguity. Mental instability in a family would no more have been hinted at than any other lapse in taste—such as the omission of, say, the McAllisters from an invitation list.

It was an impasse. Ellie was a sick girl, that much was obvious; and if she imagined that the sickness was hereditary and of the mind, then the obvious way to cure her was to prove that no such hereditary sickness existed; for some devious reason of his own, her doctor seemed unwilling to do this, managing to dismiss the idea as ridiculous, and at the same time do nothing to refute it. Yes, an impasse.

But acceptance of impasses was not what had promoted John Lamb from a humble position behind his father's junk stall in Brixton market, South London, to a half share in one of the most successful antique and decorating businesses in Paris (with forthcoming extensions in New York and Dallas). The time for breaking promises had clearly come; so, on the morning after the knife incident, he left Ellie asleep, with a note propped up on her bedside table, and went to see her brother.

Richie lived in one of the architecturally unforgivable but otherwise convenient apartment buildings on Russian Hill. Lamb was surprised to find that the décor was austere; he had outgrown the arid Scandinavian trends himself, but liked what Ellie's brother had done with them. The view, that most prized possession of all San Franciscans, was remarkable because it was a corner apartment, facing east across Telegraph Hill and the Embarcadero towards Oakland, and south across the towers of downtown towards a vista which seemed to embrace the entire length of the Bay.

Richie himself, looking recherché in a garment of Arab origin, was drinking coffee. When John Lamb reminded him of what he had said concerning Ellie and Stefan, he groaned: "I knew *that* dear little remark was going to come back and haunt me one day."

"Did you . . . Do you believe it's true?"

Richard looked out of the window at his friend's shapely and well-basted body, lying on the south-facing balcony in the surprising heat of another glittering January day. "You might think," he replied thoughtfully, "that it would be simple to go out there and ask him to tell us." He shook his head. "He'd lie, he always lies—and of course, he'd fuck a goat if the goat asked nicely enough."

"Do you think it really happened?"

"Yes. I thought so right away, as soon as I got back from that market clutching my sack of goodies."

"What kind of state was she in, Ellie?"

"She was high."

"Drunk?"

"No—she'd only had one glass of wine. It was more like an acid high. I thought . . . I don't know what I thought." He began to pace restlessly about the big bare room, biting his thumb. Stefan smiled alluringly at him through the thick glass, but was ignored. He stood staring at the Bay Bridge, leaping off on its astonishing four-mile journey across the water to Oakland. "Just how sick is she?"

"Very sick, I'm afraid."

"What does Hillier have to say?"

"A lot of words."

"Stalling?"

"Yes."

"Why?"

"How would *I* know, I'm the stranger around here! I thought you might."

Richard gave him a cold turquoise glance. "I'm worse than a stranger, I'm an Owen Spenser."

"But you've lived here a long time."

"Five years, you must be kidding! They only begin to talk to you after the first hundred—and as far as I'm concerned, they can go screw, they're a bunch of dead bores anyway." He began to prowl about the room again.

John Lamb watched him with growing disquiet—which, finally, he had to voice: "Jesus, you don't . . . you don't *believe* all that insanity crap, do you?"

Richard paused and looked at him for a long time, biting his lip, before saying, "Well, it's not a *new* story—put it that way."

"Now I suppose we're back at Aunt Leona."

"Not just Aunt Leona."

"Then what?"

Pacing again, Richard said, "I don't know, I don't remember. Maybe I never heard anything . . . definite —you know how it is in families."

Angrily, but aware that the anger was only another facet of fear, Lamb said, "It's all balls—she's no more insane than you are."

"Some yardstick!"

Unable to bear that raging restlessness, and what might lie behind it, any more, John Lamb shot out a hand and grasped the other young man's arm as he passed. "Richie, don't you start double-talking me too; I've had as much double-talk as I can take."

"For Christ's sake!" He pulled his arm free. "Can't you see I'm worried. I'm scared. I don't know what to do—where to begin."

"I do. I'm going to get at the facts—it's the only thing I *can* do. If there was . . . anything like that in your family's past, there'll be records . . ."

"Hardly a thing you take ads in the paper about."

"There'll be clues, there'll be leads."

Ellie's brother examined him carefully, analytically, head slightly on one side.

"I'm going to get at the truth."

"I'm not absolutely crazy about the truth myself."

"Sometimes it's necessary."

"And if . . . if it turns out to be what you least want to hear? It usually does."

"That's a fence I'll jump when I get to it."

Richard shook his head, but whether in surprise, disbelief, or pity, it was impossible to tell—until he said, "Well, well! Our Ellie picked herself quite a guy, she really did."

"Will you help me?"

"Sure. If I'm a nut-case as well as a faggot, I guess I may as well know it. Where do we start?"

"I've been reading some family books I got out of the house, but they were useless."

"Of course they were—there's nothing left there now. Uncle Phew handed it all over to the Lilienthal."

"What's that?"

"One of those foundation-type libraries, full of junk nobody wants to know about."

"Can you get me in?"

"If I can find my card, of course I can."

The search for the card took them to another big, bare room which was clearly used as a studio. On an easel near the window was an unfinished portrait of Stefan—the brushwork remarkably assured, the attitude of the painter sharp and humorous. Lamb was again surprised. "You?"

"Oh yes."

"It's very good."

"It's *quite* good. I'm *quite* a good writer too—out of Truman Capote by Salinger. I also play the piano *quite* well. I'm what pompous heteros like to think of, about themselves, as a Renaissance-type man; actually, we're all dilly dilettantes—in my case because I have too much bread." He stood looking at the portrait with amused contempt, and added, perhaps a trifle sadly, "It won't be finished."

"That's stupid. It really is excellent—and funny."

Richie examined the portrait with a cold blue stare which seemed to see not merely through the canvas but through its handsome subject as well. "It won't be finished because I'm giving him the push—before, if you'll forgive the unladylike expression, he gives me the pox." He held up the card, grinning. "Let's go and wake up the Lilienthal; we're probably the first customers since Henry James."

The library was housed just off Van Ness Avenue in one of the large but low-lying mansions of the Western Addition. Contrary to Richard's predictions, there were quite a number of silent and studious figures poring over San Francisco's past. The acidulous lady who greeted them, saying, "Can I help you?" in a tone of voice implying extreme doubt, changed her attitude promptly as soon as she saw the name on the card; librarians at the Lilienthal were obviously required to be social registers as well. They were even ushered into a small private room as a sign of special respect, and to them was brought, with speed and efficiency, a trolley-load of books, folders, and files.

The no-longer-acidulous lady informed them that if

they were interested in the minutiae of Spenser family life, they had better ignore the printed material; even so, they were confronted by an enormous array of journals, both public and private, diaries, letters, family trees, painstakingly neat daybooks describing journeys to Europe, account books, deeds of every kind, birth- marriage- and death-certificates, school reports, re- ports of board meetings . . . Since 1842, when "Old Dick" had first arrived in New York, the Spensers seemed to lie before them on the table with all their hopes and fears and loves and ambitions. To John Lamb there was something touching about it. Richard Owen Spenser was not touched. "Well," he said, "thank God the old boy's past was shrouded in mystery or we'd probably be wading back to 1442."

Though at first they neither of them had any idea where to start or how to use the material, they soon found that large portions of it could be laid aside immediately—everything, in fact, that dealt with the family's public, business, and financial life; the clues that they were searching for were personal, highly personal, and so it was to the diaries and journals that they resorted, using the Index to which the librarian had introduced them—and the Index itself was a booklet of some thirty pages.

Time came to a stop in the small silent room. Only a strip of sunlight moving across the carpet indicated its passing. Occasionally one or other of them would make a comment, aloud or under his breath: "Jesus, did Great-Aunt Beth *have* to write like a drunken spider crab!" or "Why do you suppose Cornelius, born 1851, went to Australia?"

"To get away from his father, I should think—he sounds a *real* bastard."

The patch of sunlight reached the edge of the carpet and began to climb laboriously up the wall, getting smaller as it did so.

"I really believe Mary, born 1881, got herself in the family way."

Richard didn't answer. He had tipped his chair back from the table and was staring at the patch of sunlight with narrowed eyes. John Lamb looked at him over Mary's diary. "What's the matter? Bored?"

Richard flashed him an absent glance. "No." He tipped the chair forward again and looked at the family tree spread out on the table in front of him. It was not the largest tree in the collection, a heavy vellum roll housed in a red-leather case which had been specially made for it, but a smaller one which Richard had found in a folder. "There's a funny thing here!" He laid a finger on the document in question, and Lamb leaned over to look at it.

Reduced to its barest branches, the shape of the tree was a simple one. Old Dick had produced, among several daughters, two sons, William and Thomas. Thomas had taken his share of Father's gold-rush fortune and had gone back to Europe, thus passing out of the picture. William had also sired two sons (as well as three daughters), and it had been these two, Owen and Harold, whose disagreements had separated the family. Owen, in Philadelphia, had produced Ellie's and Richard's father, among other children. Harold, in San Francisco, had been the father of five; and it was upon the last of these, Matthew, that Richard's finger now rested.

"What's funny about it?" He wanted to go back to Mary's diary; indeed, he thought that Richard was wasting valuable time in this prolonged study of the family tree.

"Little Matthew," said Richard, "was born on May 13, 1928."

"I can see that."

Richard moved his finger up the branch of the tree to Matthew's father; it came to rest on the date of Harold's death: May 13, 1928. "He died," said Richard thoughtfully, "on the same day his son was born. Now wouldn't you call that a coincidence?"

John Lamb experienced a tremor of excitement, and, a second later, a much more violent tremor of uneasiness. The two young men stared at each other, thinking.

"I wonder," Richard added, still thoughtful, "whether we're going to regret all this." John Lamb was wondering the same, but they both knew that for better or worse, there was no turning back. Curiosity, if no nobler emotion, was driving them forward to the end.

Hesitantly, Lamb said, "What . . . are you thinking?"

"I'm not *thinking* anything. I happen to know, because it's an accepted piece of San Francisco history, that Harold Spenser shot himself."

There was a sudden dead stillness in the impersonal little room. After a time Richard added, "But I never knew he did it on the day his youngest son was born—and I don't think anybody else does either."

They stared at each other again. Something very unpleasant had entered the room quietly, and now sat invisible in the corner. Richard put his finger back on the family tree and John Lamb saw all too clearly what he was indicating. Little Matthew, on whose birth day his father had committed suicide, had himself lived no longer than thirty-six hours. Richard's finger moved across the chart. Matthew had had two sisters and two brothers. Patrick, born in 1925, had died at the age of seven. Catherine, born in 1921, had been killed in London during the Second World War as a result of German bombing. It was the other two that held John Lamb's attention: Hugh, who had died unmarried at the age of sixty, and who had—he remembered now— fallen foul of the law for molesting a little girl, and Leona, who had been certified insane, who was still locked up in an institution. He realized that he had broken out all over in a chill sweat. Richard said, "I've had enough of this—I need some fresh air."

Emerging from the library, they walked for some time in silence, each lost in his own thoughts, which could only be concerned with the alarming implications of what they had just seen. After a time Richard indicated a bar which they happened to be passing; John Lamb nodded agreement, and they went in.

Richard took a gulp of the strong Scotch he had ordered and said, "Well—do you want to tell me what you're thinking? Or shall I tell you what I'm thinking?"

Lamb did not particularly want to think about it at all. He could not get the picture of Ellie out of his mind—Ellie lying so unnaturally inert upon her rumpled bed, staring out of the window with lackluster eyes which he could at times hardly recognize. He sighed and said, "You tell me."

Richard rubbed a hand over his face, took another big drink of whiskey, and said, "I'm thinking . . . that

here is this man called Harold Spenser—third-genera-
tion rich, strong-minded, clever, intelligent, happily
married . . . He was married to a great beauty, by the
way—Stella Bellfort—even richer than he was. Anyway, here he is: the man who has everything, including
four fine children . . ."

"Five."

Richard shook his head. "The youngest hasn't been
born yet."

"Oh Christ, I see what you mean."

"On May 13, 1928, his beautiful wife gives birth to
another child, a third boy—and this boy . . ." His
voice limped to a halt; after a moment's pause he
forced it to go on, with an obvious effort: "This boy is
. . . Oh God, I don't know—a monster perhaps, cre-
tinous, it only lived a few hours. Maybe the doctor's
told him outright what was wrong, maybe he already
suspected, because one of his daughters, Leona, wasn't
right in the head—there'd even been talk of putting her
away.

"He was a very proud man, very conscious of his
position in the city, very conscious of family, and he'd
. . . he'd produced a family with insanity running clear
through it! I guess he just . . . couldn't take it; he blew
his brains out. And the only remaining son, Hugh—
who wasn't homosexual or anything, I assure you—
lived to be sixty, and never dared to get married
because his sister was in a nuthouse and he knew what
he'd . . . inherited."

Most men don't realize how thoroughly they live on
hope until hope withdraws itself; either hope does this
very seldom or mankind is very stupid, otherwise we

would live in a welter of despair. Hope withdrew from John Lamb in a shabby bar in San Francisco, and nothing that his natural optimism, his belief in reason, or his courage could do about it made any difference at all. He tried to tell himself that the whole thing was pure guesswork, but the cold fact was that two such disparate people as himself and Richard had made identical guesses; he reasoned with himself that the whole thing would have to be checked and rechecked, but even as he did so, another colder reason piled up hideous facts against him: Ellie's uncharacteristic apathy, her sudden newly acquired clumsiness, the way she now had of seeming to be elsewhere, listening to voices which he could not hear; and Dr. Hillier's vagueness—couldn't that simply have been the reaction of a kindly man to the fate which had overtaken a pair of young lovers?

His stomach had turned to lead inside him; he felt physically sick, and hoped that he might evade actual vomiting, since he doubted if his legs would get him as far as the toilet.

He turned and looked at Ellie's brother, and found that this indefatigable young man had suddenly aged ten years; had shrunk into himself. He wanted to say something—something comforting—but his brain had ceased to serve him. After a moment Richie, aware of his regard, also turned, and their eyes met in a bleak stare.

Afterwards he was never to know what actually triggered the thought. Was it the hard, utterly sane brilliance of those blue eyes which were exactly like Ellie's? Perhaps. His brain seemed to explode inside his cranium; he could well have believed that like the man in the comic strip, stars might be seen leaping from his head. He shouted, *"No!"* in such a loud voice that the other people in the bar all turned as one man to stare at him. "Richie, we're out of our minds." It wasn't the happiest phrase to choose in the circumstances. Richard stared. He went on, tripping over words in his excitement: "Does your father have brothers and sisters?"

"One of each."

"Are *they* mentally defective?"

"It doesn't necessarily show in every generation—in fact, it—"

"*Are* they?"

"Not as far as I know."

"Of course they're not—and neither is your father, and neither was your Grandfather Owen. Neither was his brother, Harold. Don't you *see?* We've been jumping to conclusions just because Harold shot himself." He grabbed the other young man's arm and shook him so hard that he nearly fell off his barstool. "Richie, it didn't have to be your family at all, it could have been *her!*"

Still staring, Richard Owen Spenser said, "Stella Bellfort. Jesus Christ!"

"Harold's children may have been as mad as March hares, every single one of them, but the Owen Spensers are . . . are as sane as I am."

Richie had to admit to himself that though his possible brother-in-law didn't look in the least sane at that particular moment, he was in fact one of the sanest, as well as one of the most determined, young men he ever expected to meet.

Suddenly they were both out of the bar and running.

The little room in the Lilienthal Library was exactly as they had left it; they pounced on the litter of books and papers. Richard seized the diary of Beth, whose writing was that of a spider crab. "*She* doesn't leave out a darn thing—she was describing how Harold had fallen in love, when I put her down."

From the Index, Lamb said, "Is that Elizabeth Maud, born 1885?"

"That's her."

"It says here there are five volumes."

"Then it has to be Number Three—this one ends before the engagement." He began to search the closely packed trolley.

Still in the Index, Lamb said, "If you find the Bellfort Letters, bound, I'll have a go at them."

Richard straightened up, holding all the diaries. He looked up from them, frowning.

"What's the matter?"

Richard held out the diaries so that he could see them. They were numbered One, Two, Four and Five. Number Three was missing. They searched thoroughly through all the material, but could not find it. Ten minutes later, while Lamb, swearing, was looking for the Bellfort Letters, Richie picked up the Index and examined it carefully. Eventually he said, "John—don't bother."

Lamb looked up at him, surprised. Richard showed him the Index. Against the third volume of Elizabeth Maud's diary there was a neatly penciled asterisk. There was another against the Daybook of Sarah Rose, Elizabeth Maud's sister—another against a folder of correspondence entitled "Family Dispute between Harold and Owen Spenser." There was, they found, an asterisk against every document which had any bearing at all on Stella Bellfort. A note on the last page of the Index explained their meaning: "Books marked thus have been withdrawn from the collection by family request."

"Whose request?" shouted Richard Owen Spenser at the librarian on duty.

"For Christ's sake, *whose* request?" he demanded of the assistant librarian, who had been rudely awakened from his usual afternoon doze.

"I don't give a shit," he hissed at the deputy head librarian over the telephone, "what the rules of the fucking place are. I know darn well my *father* never asked for the stuff to be removed, and he's head of the family. My Uncle Edward is a priest employed by the Vatican, and if he's ever heard of the Lilienthal, I'll eat my hat. My Aunt Rose is married to an English baronet, and hasn't been back to San Francisco for thirty years—and that leaves me, and I certainly never requested anything. So it comes back to the Bellforts, doesn't it?" He silenced an uncertain mutter on the other end of the line by shouting, "Will you tell me by what authority any Bellfort can remove *my* property from this library without my consent?"

The deputy head librarian could apparently not answer this. Richie said, "Think it over. And while you're about it, I advise you to get your attorney to think it over too."

They swept out, past various amazed and bemused faces, got into Richie's car, and headed for Dr. Robert Hillier.

"Jesus," said Richie through his teeth, "I'll teach

these sons of bitches to go scaring the shit out of people!''

It seemed that on two afternoons a week Dr. Hillier was in residence for private consultation at his surgery near the junction of Powell and Sutter streets. This, according to Richie, made him more discreetly available to those of his patients who didn't want their particular condition to be known to all and sundry on Pacific or Presidio Heights. The doctor, who had just finished making arrangements for a young lady following some pretty stupid miscalculations with the pill, was on the point of leaving for home, a cup of tea, and the latest number of his favorite yachting magazine, which had arrived that morning from England. His nurse, who had already been given her instructions, said, "I'm so sorry—Dr. Hillier won't be seeing any more patients this afternoon.''

"That suits me fine,'' snapped Richard, "because we don't happen to be patients. Please tell him Mr. Owen Spenser is here.'' When she had withdrawn he gave John Lamb a chill conspiratorial smile and added, "It's not for nothing they call me Bitchy Richie around the bars—leave this to me, huh?''

The doctor received them with bland affability, which didn't quite hide the edges of uneasiness. "Well now, fellers, what can I do for you?''

"For a start,'' replied Richard, at his most acid, "you can explain a remark you made about my sister a little over a week ago when we called you in the middle of the night.''

Hillier didn't like the tone, but controlled himself admirably, even managing a smile. "I hope I'm going to remember the context.''

"If you don't, you may go down in medical history as the doctor with the worst memory ever."

Hillier flushed angrily, but Richard gave him no time to speak. "You were saying that you were against consulting a psychiatrist about my sister's condition because, after a few sessions of psychiatric messing around—and these are your very words—'that nice, beautiful, and above all, *healthy* girl over there is going to imagine she's some kind of nut-case.'"

Dr. Hillier's expression made it very clear that he remembered this as clearly as Richie did.

"Perhaps you could explain exactly what that meant?"

"It was merely an opinion—not a very unusual one, many people share it."

"The only unusual thing about it," said Ellie's brother evenly, "is that she now *does* imagine herself to be some kind of nut-case, as you well know, because John here told you all about it."

Anger showing through a little now, the doctor said, "Richie, if you're not satisfied with my services as a physician . . ."

"We haven't yet *had* your services as a physician—only as a secret agent for what they call the Establishment."

"I've no intention of losing my temper with you. Our families have been friendly . . ."

"Fuck our families!" replied Richard Owen Spenser with quiet venom. "I think you *know* what may be wrong with Ellie. I think, and I thought at the time, you had a nasty suspicion about it the night we first called you in to attend her. I think it scared you shitless, and I think you've been stalling ever since that night because our great-grandfathers used to drink champagne out of the same whore's lousy stinking slipper at the old Poodle Dog way back in the days when men were men."

Something in this—and something beyond the mere venom, John Lamb was inclined to think—had hit Dr. Robert Hillier where it hurt. Fumblingly, he said, "I thought . . . that we all agreed that your sister's ah . . . condition was not one that called for . . . for publicity."

"I'm not asking for publicity, Dr. Hillier, I'm asking *you* to say what you think is the matter with her."

"I already told you—I don't know."

"Oh, but I think you do; and I'll tell you why—because something like it happened before."

"What are you talking about? The other night was the first time I ever attended Ellie, and you know it."

"I didn't say that it happened to Ellie before. To some other member of the family."

"Now Richard, wait a minute . . . !" The mental contortions which Dr. Hillier was having to employ in order to wriggle out of this trap were almost visible to the naked eye. "I started practicing in '52. By that time there was only one member of your family around, your Uncle Hugh, and he always consulted Dr. Carrington because they were old friends—went to the same college, I believe."

Lamb glanced at Richard, wondering if he had talked himself out of the argument. An answering blue glint told him that Bitchy Richie still held a trump card—which he now proceeded to play: "Dr. Hillier, I may be only an *Owen* Spenser from Back East, but I'm not a moron, and if it comes to it, I can play Happy Families with the best of you up there on your dreary little old hill, and even out in the far-flung suburbia of Burlingame. Your wife was Betty Macfadden, and her father was Dr. Ian Macfadden, and he must have started practicing soon after the earthquake in '06, and if there's anything *he* didn't know about the Spensers, it could easily be written on the head of a pin . . ."

"Just because my father-in-law happened to be the family physician to . . ."

"I also happen to know that you were his faithful assistant for five years before he retired. Dig?"

It was clear from Robert Hillier's expression that he understood completely. For good measure, however, Bitchy Richie delivered one last stomach punch: "In case you don't know where to start, there's always the grand old name of Bellfort, isn't there? Forgive me for not crossing myself when I speak it!"

Three

BETTY HILLIER said, "You look worried, dear; is anything the matter?"

Her husband was lying in his favorite wing-backed chair, his favorite yachting magazine lying unopened on his knee, and his favorite highball resposing, un-sipped, at his elbow. He said, "No, dear. Just tired, I guess."

From long habit he made a point of never telling his wife what interested him, worried him, or indeed occupied him professionally; she was a compulsive gossip. He drank a little of the highball and opened the magazine, not even seeing its usually succulent pages. Betty Hillier was writing letters; she wrote a great many letters; all forms of communication were the breath of life to her; the Hillier telephone bill was always enormous.

After a while, when he judged it safe, her husband said very casually, "I met the young Owen Spenser boy today, he seems quite a nice kid."

"Really? I always heard he was . . . you know, one of those."

"That doesn't matter much these days, does it?"

Betty Hillier laughed fondly. He knew that she was in the habit of saying to her clucking cronies, "Robert is

so broad-minded, you know—but then, being a doctor . . .''

Ever more casual, he said, "I don't remember the
Harold Spensers, not even as a kid—I guess we never
knew them too well." There were certain areas in
which he had to be exceedingly diplomatic; his wife
was six years his senior, and didn't like to be reminded
of the fact.

"Well, they were a lot *older* than I was, of course."

"Oh yes, of course."

"Poor Hugh was a young man while I was just a little
girl. He was very good-looking then; dozens of girls
would have married him at the drop of a hat. Such a
pity—all that money and that huge house! I still can't
believe he was really . . . doing what they said he was
doing with that child. I can't even believe it was really
Hugh, that fat sloppy old man!" She sighed deeply. "Oh
dear, life is *cruel* sometimes!"

"Then there was a sister who was killed in the war."

"Catherine. She was a *strange* one!"

"How come she was killed?"

"The bombing in London. God knows what she was
doing in London, I don't ever remember hearing. Some
man, I suppose."

"Why? Did she go for men a lot?"

"They all did, all those Spenser girls: got it from their
mother, I suppose." She fell into reverie, biting the end
of her pen, so that her husband was forced to prod her.
There were things here he needed, perhaps desperately,
to know. "How do you mean 'strange'?"

"Catherine? I don't know, really. She was only five
years older than I was, but you know how it is with
kids. There's a gulf between ten and fifteen. By the time

you're all fortyish, it doesn't matter a rap. Maybe not so much strange as . . . sly. Uncomfortable. Leona was the same—poor Leona—but then, *she* wasn't quite right in the head. Something to do with her birth—I remember father saying it was one of the most difficult he'd ever attended."

Robert Hillier sighed. He knew that he was only putting off the moment when he would have to go downstairs to his study and drag that heavy old filing cabinet out of the closet where he had kept it all these years. He wished very much indeed that he had *not* kept it, but there it sat in musty darkness, and if he listened carefully, he could hear it calling out to him, quietly but insistently, with a slight Scottish accent— the accent of his father-in-law, whom he had loved. In all, he had only consulted it half a dozen times in fifteen years, and it had only proved to be useful once—in the case of Janie Freeman's asthma. Now, suddenly, during the past days it had become synonymous with his conscience. Robert Hillier, who liked the easy life only a little less than he liked his sailing boat, thought it monstrously unfair that he should suffer from a conscience when most of his colleagues so very patently did not.

"I suppose you could say they were *all* strange," said his wife reflectively. "Strange and . . . exotic in a way. They used to make everyone else seem rather dull. Their parties were always special. The others were all alike, you could hardly remember sometimes just whose house you were in, but the Harold Spensers always thought of something new and exciting. Nobody could quite believe it when he suddenly shot himself—you remember that, of course."

"Yes, of course. Though I never did hear why."

"There were dozens of stories, but none of them made any sense."

"Something to do with a woman, they said."

"No, no—that was just stupid uninformed gossip."

"What did your father think?"

Betty Hillier frowned at the opal evening outside the window. "Father was very upset; I'd never seen him so upset by anything. I think maybe he spoke about it to Mother, but not to me."

Again her husband heard the faint voice of the old filing cabinet, calling, muffled, from its dusty closet in the corner of his study.

Betty Hillier said, "Some people went around saying he'd caught . . . a disease."

"Syphilis, I suppose." He could never understand why gossiping women like his wife, who gloried in the most obscene details of other people's lives, could yet be so pernickety about ordinary honest words.

She gave a tiny shudder. "Yes. And some people said he'd done something crazy on the stock market and lost all his money."

"That's not likely—they're still loaded."

"People said that was *her* money . . ." He had noticed before that when the thought of Stella Spenser crossed the mind of anybody who had known her, even remotely, it short-circuited all other connections; his wife was no exception: "Oh boy! She was *really* something, was Stella Harold Spenser—I really do believe she was the most beautiful woman I ever saw in my whole life. Men used to go absolutely *crazy* about her . . ."

"Maybe that's what made her husband shoot himself."

"Oh *no!*" Betty Hillier was appalled. One of the nicer things about her, he always thought, was that parallel with her insatiable appetite for the dirt ran an almost religious admiration for what was truly good in people. "Stella adored that man, everybody said so, even my mother, and she didn't like her at all."

"Why not?"

"Because Father was so crazy about her, I guess. He worshiped the ground she walked on, you know, and he knew *all* about her because he was her doctor."

"Doctors," her husband replied dryly, "don't always know everything about their beautiful women patients."

"He was her friend, too, a good friend. He stuck by her even when . . . when a lot of other people wouldn't even speak to her."

"Oh! Why was that?"

"When he shot himself she went mad with grief; I don't think she ever recovered, not really. All the . . . silly things she did later, with men I mean, were because she didn't care any more."

Robert Hillier had naturally heard about the behavior of Stella Harold Spenser following her husband's death; it was a well-mulled tale in certain circles and had, over the years, lost nothing in the telling. However, it suited him at this moment to continue in ignorance: "Made a fool of herself, did she?"

"You'd better believe it—all over Europe."

"That's funny—I thought she married again."

"She did. In the end. But he was *years* younger than

she was—oh, he was a simply *gorgeous*-looking man, all us kids were crazy about him. But they didn't like it here—too much back-biting, I guess; they went back to Europe. She died there. I don't know what happened to him—he wasn't good family. Why are you so interested suddenly?"

"I told you, I met the *Owen* Spenser boy this afternoon."

"They say he's just too much! And Marianne told me that the sister is living . . . you know, quite openly with some young man; she has that studio in back of the big house."

"They're getting married, I believe."

"Well, they'd better do it quick, the things people are saying!"

The filing cabinet—black, chipped, a little rusty here and there—stared him full in the face now. He sighed deeply and stood up. "Got a little work to do before dinner."

"Don't forget we're going to the Fieldings'."

"As if I could!" He took his drink, walked out of the room, along the softly carpeted hall and down the sharply twisting paneled staircase decorated with photographs of yachts he had known and loved, to his study. He put his drink on the desk, switched on lights, went to the neatly concealed row of closets which ran along the whole of one wall, their doors adapted to fit the paneling, and opened the one in the corner. It struck him for the first time that the filing cabinet—sturdy, practical, battered by time, and full of carefully observed and carefully stored knowledge—was very like his father-in-law, whose pride and joy it had been. He remembered also that once, many years ago, in the

days when he too had still been in love with the magical
arts of healing and medicine, he had even thought that
he would edit his father-in-law's case histories, making
them carefully anonymous in the process, and publish
them as a memorial to the remarkable old doctor whom
he had loved. "Later," he told himself. "Later, when
I've made my money and have the time." Here, on
another level, the ancient filing cabinet assaulted his
conscience yet again.

He found the key, unlocked the bar-mechanism
which, running the height of the thing, released all its
drawers, and opened the top one. The sight of the
meticulous handwriting tugged at his heart. The neat
index informed him, under Si- to Sp-, that his father-in-
law had at one time or another treated no less than
fourteen Spensers, both of the Harold and Owen
variety. Looking at them—Charles, Elizabeth Maud,
Stella, Hugh, Matthew—he heard again the voice of
Richard Owen in his office, speaking with quiet venom:
"I think you *know* what may be wrong with Ellie. I
think you had a nasty suspicion about it the night we
first called you in to attend her . . ."

Was it true? In a way, yes. He couldn't remember
which of the things had been told him by old Dr.
Macfadden and which he had heard, as mere gossip,
since—but he couldn't deny that it was, in essence,
true; he was fundamentally a lazy man who had long
ago fallen out of love with medicine, and he had
developed a hundred devious ways of evading the total
involvement which medicine, the insatiable mistress,
demanded of her men; as soon as he had seen Ellie
Owen Spenser writhing on that bed, the automatic
defense mechanism which had become part of his

being had immediately begun to search about for ways of escape; when the young Englishman had come here, to this room, to recount the girl's fears, he had tried not to listen with more than his ears, and had fled away to his boat and a day's sailing, which he pretended to have enjoyed as much as any other, but which had, in reality, been flawed by the knowledge of his own selfishness, the taunting of the discarded mistress, the jibes of his maddening conscience.

Well, they'd all caught up with him now. Beyond the voice of that odd, angry young homosexual shouting at him in his own office, he had seemed to hear the gentle voice of his father-in-law berating him for a world of broken trust. He reached out and pulled open the drawer of the file marked Si- to Sp-. The names flashed past his eyes: Silverman . . . Sirral . . . Soames . . . Sommers . . . Sopwith . . . Sparrington . . . Spears . . . Spender . . . Spenser . . .

The cards flickered to a stop; Robert Hillier stood there, staring, his mouth slightly open; he went back to Spellman and tried again. Spenser. There was nothing —merely the section card with the name neatly printed on its projecting tongue in his father-in-law's tidy capital letters. Of the fourteen case sheets, no sign.

How long had they been missing? There was no way of telling, but presumably ever since the filing cabinet had come into his possession at Dr. Macfadden's death. Since then he had only referred to the system half a dozen times, and never to the Spenser section—somewhat naturally, considering that he himself had never, until the other night, had a Spenser for a patient.

Initially, under the influence of that lazy selfishness which had long ago become second nature to him, he had felt a cowardly surge of relief, but this was very swiftly swept away by a much larger wave of apprehension, for this was a situation from which there was no escape; impossible to close the cabinet, go upstairs, help himself to another drink before taking a shower and spending the evening swapping inanities with Jack and Vera Fielding; this was a situation in which he was already, and deeply, involved.

As if to make sure of this involvement, his eye now settled on something blue which protruded slightly beyond the edge of the neatly arranged cards in the file—which protruded, now that he looked closer, from behind the yellowing section card marked "Spenser." He put his hand into the gap once occupied by the fourteen missing case histories and drew out an envelope; on it, in his father-in-law's writing, was his own name. Robert Hillier sighed. So it had in fact been the old man's voice which he had heard that afternoon, echoing in hollow counterpart to the stinging words of Richard Owen Spenser, "Fuck our families!"—yes, but the association between them was more alive than the mere memory of great-grandfathers drinking champagne out of a whore's slipper: so real that unless he was very much mistaken he could actually feel it between his fingers at that moment, in the shape of handsome blue stationery, faded only a little with age. He slit the envelope, pulled out two closely covered pages of notepaper, and read:

11 June 1956.

My dear Robert,
If you ever read this letter, two things are relatively certain—as certain as anything may be in this very uncertain

life. (1) I shall be dead, or I'd be telling you in person what's written here. (2) You have been called upon to attend one of the Spenser family in a professional capacity.

As you're very well aware, these case histories have been one of the ruling passions of my life. The older I get, and the more of them that I file here, the more I seem to see in them a kind of common denominator. (Unfortunately, I would need another hundred years or so in order to discover if I am correct.) I mention this because I want you to know, if you haven't already guessed it, that I have removed all reference to the Spensers with regret and against my better judgment. I've done so only because very strong pressure has been brought to bear on me from within the family itself.

The original demand was that I destroy all the Spenser case histories, but I refused to do this; and in refusing, I was thinking mainly of you. If you've come to this file, it can only be because you need to know something pretty badly; and I can make a darned shrewd guess what that may be. I know the Harold Spensers well—too well, I've often thought.

The family argued that much of what was filed here could cause great trouble and distress if it fell into the wrong hands. I argued that this is true of the whole file: of the records of any physician who has ever bothered to keep them. I argued that in the right hands, which is to say in the hands of some other doctor, what was filed here might help *alleviate* trouble and distress.

This was not an argument that they were able to refute. I won my point, but only on the condition that I place the case histories in a safety deposit box in my bank, which as you know is the Two Oceans, Montgomery Street. You'll find the key of the box in a sealed envelope at the bottom of this cabinet, in the section marked Miscellaneous.

> Your ever affectionate father-in-law,
> Ian Macfadden

P.S. I have just remembered that you once had the rather flattering idea that you might, at some future date, edit these papers for publication; though I very much doubt, my dear Robert, that you will ever have the time for this considerable task. If it is that—or any other reason, barring fundamental medical necessity—which has placed this letter in your hand, I urge you not to go to the bank and not to open that box. Everything in it is much better forgotten.

Robert Hillier took the letter to his desk and sat down, placing it on the blotter in front of him. Then he drank what remained of his highball. Then he read the letter through again, slowly and carefully. *If you've come to this file, it can only be because you need to know something pretty badly; and I can make a darned shrewd guess what that may be . . . I urge you not to go to the bank and not to open that box. Everything in it is much better forgotten . . . Very strong pressure has been brought to bear on me from within the family itself . . . I know the Harold Spensers well—too well, I've often thought.*

He rested his head in his hands and closed his eyes. He was overcome with the absolute certainty that if he opened them and looked up, he would find the old man sitting in the chair by the fireplace where he had always liked to sit during the last years of retirement, talking of this and that with his son-in-law. (And how well he had understood that son-in-law! *I very much doubt, my dear Robert, that you will ever have the time for this considerable task.*) He was sure that if he looked up he would find the honest grey eyes—as grey and as uncompromising as that northern sea from the shores of which his family had originally come—fixed on him with amused interest; and the amused and interested voice would say, "What are you going to do, Robert?"

John Lamb and Richie, riding on that odd mixture of elation, anger, and frustration which the discoveries and evasions of the afternoon had aroused in them, decided that the best thing to do with Ellie was to take her by storm. They burst in upon her waving two bottles of champagne and a jar of caviar, and babbling about this great Greek place which had just opened down in the Western Addition where the music was the best this side of Athens and the waiters (according to Richie) not only ravishing one and all but willing into the bargain.

Ellie, who had been lying on the sofa, staring out of the window, her mind virtually blank, was at first almost angry with them for disturbing her vegetable peace; but she quickly realized that they were not going to take no for an answer. Less quickly, because of the strange, sluggish nature of her intelligence these days, she realized that they had stumbled upon evidence which, in their opinion at any rate, made all her fears of insanity look ridiculous.

By this time Richard had dragged her into the bathroom, pushed her down in front of the mirror and was seeing to her hair, which, he said, would have disgraced an English sheepdog in a rainstorm. Lamb, meanwhile, kept them both supplied with glasses of champagne and mouthfuls of caviar on oyster crackers.

Within a half-hour Richie had dried and combed the hair, reorganized her face, zipped her into one of her favorite dresses from Paris, and the three of them were jammed into the front seat of his car on their way to Niko's Taverna, which turned out to be all that he had promised, and more.

The place was full—a great many young people—the music was indeed excellent—that odd mixture of mournful cadences and stomping rhythms which so exactly mirrors the Greek character; the food was good, the retsina delicious, and the waiters friendly and funny.

Amid all this din and movement they explained to Ellie more carefully the things they had discovered at the Lilienthal. Just what her reaction was, it was hard for them to tell, because in some extraordinary way she seemed to have left the girl who had been so obsessed by these things behind in the stable-studio. The Ellie who now sat between them, stowing away large quantities of mushrooms and onions à la Grecque, was the old Ellie whom John Lamb had known and loved in Paris. In one single hour she had changed completely; whether this change was a direct result of what they had been telling her, or simply, at last, a recovery from the sickness that had attacked her, was open to doubt. In a sense it no longer mattered to either of them. A great shadow had lifted—though there was some rough accounting yet to be done—the Ellie they both loved had come back to them, and they were young: young and laughing in a happy place which was full of chatter and music and singing and (that peculiarly Greek form of emotional release) the smashing of cheap plates.

In the quiet, heavily curtained library of 337 Gilman Street, Amelia Guardi and Lulu Jenkins sat on either side of the table, looking at the tape recorder. From the neat, almost clinical black-and-steel face of the machine came the sounds of sexual intercourse; an observer would have found it partly absurd and partly obscene; what the two listening women found it, the observer would have been unable to guess; each in her own way, the two faces were quite without expression.

The noises emerging from the speaker were not in fact the whole of intercourse, since the voice that gasped and moaned and whispered endearments in a growing crescendo was simply that of a woman or girl, but the performance was so graphically real that the listening ear instinctively supplied for itself the missing elements: the grunting of the man as his climax approached, and perhaps the protesting of belabored bedsprings. "Oh Mikey," the girl gasped. "Oh Mikey, oh my God . . . Oh!"

When the whole thing had reached its peak and toppled over the abyss into sighing and silence, Mrs. Guardi leaned forward and switched off the machine. "Remarkable!"

Lulu sniffed.

Mrs. Guardi consulted her black notebook. "The girl appears to have been called Lyn, or Lynne, or possibly Lynette—did you notice that?"

Lulu nodded; she was unusually reserved tonight, seeming to be worried about something. From experience, Amelia Guardi said, "Is it indigestion again?" She had eaten her enormous helping of crab much too fast. But no, it was apparently not indigestion. Mrs. Guardi continued to pinpoint facts calmly; she had noticed that the sound of her voice, whether actual sense was being made of it or not, seemed to have a soothing effect: "Of course you remember how Stella—we must take it for granted now, I think, that the weeping woman is definitely Stella . . . how Stella shouted at him to get out of her room and take his bribery with him. When she . . . you said that, you pushed the Fabergé away from you quite violently, you know; I only just managed to stop it falling onto the floor. It seemed likely that he had actually given her the piece, and in any case, it was a lead worth following. We must always corroborate such details in real life, of course. Our whole case will depend on corroboration in the end. So I called a jeweler I happen to know in New York . . ."

Lulu stared at her, tiny mouth ajar in the shapeless wastes of her face; this meant that she was genuinely interested in, more, fascinated by, what she was being told.

"He called me back this evening, and it's all perfectly true, it all fits." She consulted her notebook. "The egg was bought from the Degroot Gallery on Madison Avenue, on November 4, 1937, by Mr. Michael Burke— that was her second husband, remember?"

"Mikey."

"Yes. In 1937 she would have been forty-two—he was twenty-three." She gave a short, sharp sigh. "Some women never learn, do they?"

As before, Lulu said, "Many women." But this time she deigned to clarify it a little. "That Michael, he had many women."

Amelia Guardi stood up and began to pace about the room, her beautiful housecoat, in a rich shade of burnt-orange velvet, glowing in the dark corners. "Lulu, Michael Burke is the . . . the crux of our problem, I feel it very strongly. Everything you've shown me strengthens the likelihood; everything points to him." She came back to the table and fixed fat Mrs. Jenkins with her powerful eyes. "The blood—whatever it is that permeates this house so strongly. The thing we are searching for—the thing we must find to prove our case. It lies in *him*—don't you feel that yourself?"

Lulu was silent for a time. Then she nodded, looking at her own odd chippolata-fingers. "He's . . . strong, he's dark—dark blue and red. Black sometimes. Not all evil. Selfish—but all men are selfish . . ." She seemed to be talking to herself. Knowing the tone, Mrs. Guardi took the candle from the bookcase and placed it on the table.

"We must make contact with him. There must be ways."

"He is always there."

"Can you try? Can you try very, very hard?"

Lulu, staring drowsily at the straight flame of the candle, said, "They don't do as *we* wish. We aren't any more important than they are. We all . . . exist side by side in time." It was one of her more astonishing occasional statements. Mrs. Guardi was duly astonished, caught with the Fabergé Easter egg in one hand—staring.

Lulu said, "Tonight is . . . different."

"What do you mean, different?"

There was no answer for a long time; then: "She, the girl, isn't there."

"Maybe that will be better for us; it's Michael we must reach." And because Lulu had sagged deep into her chair, she leaned forward, trying to impress it on

the already receding everyday intelligence: "Michael.
Mikey."

Lulu shifted uneasily in her chair, frowning at the
candle flame. "Far away," she said vaguely. And later:
"The girl isn't there . . . Stella . . . Catherine . . ."
And later still, in an irritated tone: "No, no, no!"

It took her a long time to settle down—a longer time
than Amelia Guardi had ever had to wait. Twice she
even switched off the tape recorder because it was
recording nothing.

At last, after nearly an hour, the big woman sighed
deeply and her eyes closed slowly until they were mere
slits. Mrs. Guardi switched on the recorder again,
though she was far from sure that Lulu had not simply
fallen asleep.

This was not the case. Lulu was entering into the
flame of the candle—into the inmost blue heart of the
pure flame where time and space, as the tiny, crabbed
mind of man understands them, cease to exist. Within
the small blue heart of the flame existed true time: vast
aeons and arcs of wheeling time, a chaos of time
running in every conceivable direction, obeying its own
cosmic laws—beyond the reach of man's intelligence
(but possibly not of his lost instincts)—the antithesis of
his little clock: tick-tock, tick-tock, measuring out his
little span from the womb to the tomb.

In this chaos, led by something in the house where
she was sitting, and by something in the jeweled Easter
egg on which her fat hand rested, the extraordinary
mind of Lulu Jenkins walked unerringly and beyond
fear until, wedged, as it were, between the Battle of
Waterloo and a Neanderthal man trying to learn how to

dig a hole in the ground, she came upon the Harold
Spenser family having tea on the lawn under the five
tall cypresses.

It was night now, and there was music. "When my
baby walks down the street, all the little birdies go
tweet-tweet-tweet . . ." And in the dark corridor,
music far away, the young man clutches the girl, his
body already writhing against hers as if already he was
bearing her down into the bed.

Mrs. Guardi leaned forward a little as the muffled
voice, giggling a little, whispered, "Oh Mikey, *no!* Ooh,
you are wicked. No, Mikey, please—somebody may
see."

Somebody *was* seeing. Who? Where? A shadow at
the far end of the corridor. A man? A girl? Watching.

"Who's that? Who's there? No, Mikey, really—there
was someone there, I *know* there was someone there."

But the big, strong young body, ever-lustful—except
for the thin carefully preserved body of his elderly
wife—is pushing her against a half-open door. "No,
Mikey! Somebody saw . . ." Pushing, kissing, thrust-
ing, fumbling, onto the bed.

Mrs. Guardi, leaning forward, said, "Michael? Mikey,
is that you?"

From the flaccid face opposite her came a maddening
giggle, and a child's voice said, "Everybody watch
Leona! Leona's going to stand on her head."

Amelia Guardi, slender hands tense and white as
they gripped the edge of the table, hissed, "Michael,
you were there, I know you were there. Come back. We
must speak to you."

The voice of Stella Harold Spenser, acidly venomous,
shouted, "Okay, I'll divorce you—how about that? I'll

throw you out of this house with only the clothes you stand up in. Then what? Back to the Via Veneto—back to hawking that *thing* up and down the Via Veneto! You're not as pretty as you were, but no doubt some old faggot'll fancy you!''

And then she was alone again, walking to and fro, to and fro in the big circular room with the red walls, under the hard stone eyes of the three grinning satyrs that topped the arches. Weeping again—always weeping.

The sound of this weeping seemed to enrage Amelia Guardi; in fact, the whole formless ragbag of an evening was enraging her.

"Piggy's balloon is bigger than Leona's—yah, yah, yah."

Mrs. Guardi would have liked to switch off the recorder and bring Lulu Jenkins back to the present, but she knew that the latter was impossible and that the attempt might even be dangerous; so she sat, containing her irritation, while the scrapbook of Spenser inanities continued.

"Oh Catherine, *please* play mah-jong with me. Aunt Beth, will *you* play mah-jong with me? Won't *anyone* play mah-jong with me—it's raining."

Irritated and bored, Mrs. Guardi quite clearly heard Richard Owen Spenser's car turn under the archway leading to the stable yard. It stopped. Young voices were raised in laughter: the voice of the English boy—then Ellie's voice saying, "No, I did not—that was at Vincennes."

At the same moment Mrs. Guardi also became aware of the fact that Lulu's breathing had quickened. From her lips came a voice which the other woman could not quite place; full of breathless horror, it said, "For Christ's sake, *don't touch anything*. Look, it's all over your hands—look at your hands, for Christ's sake . . ."

Ellie, first up the stairs, unlocked her front door, pushed it open, and switched on the lights. As she screamed she reeled back so abruptly that Lamb, behind her, was nearly knocked down the steep stairs. He just managed to brace himself, catching her, holding her quivering, struggling body.

"Ellie, what's the matter—what is it?"

"Look!" she was gasping. "Oh for Christ's sake, *look!*"

Lamb looked, and saw beyond her bowed, trembling head the familiar room looking as it always looked. Richie had now come up the stairs behind them. Lamb said, "What? There's no one there, darling."

Trembling, her voice coming in shocked gasps, Ellie managed to say, "Blood. Blood, all over . . . everything." She held up her two hands, gazing at their innocent whiteness in horror. "I . . . could even *feel* it."

Above them, in a shadowed angle of the big house, a window opened quietly. Mrs. Guardi stood looking down at the three figures grouped on the wooden stairs. Richard pushed past his sister and her lover, going into the room. He said, "There's nothing. Ellie, come and look, honey, there's nothing."

The girl refused to move, clinging to John Lamb and repeating the one word, "Blood. Blood. I saw it, I *felt* it on my fingers."

Lamb took her firmly by the shoulders and half

pushed, half carried her through the door. As they disappeared from sight he was saying, "Look, my darling, please look—there's nothing, nothing at all."

Amelia Guardi closed the window and went back along the corridor, through a door covered in red baize, across the hall and back into the library. Lulu, slumped deep in her chair, was muttering, "No, no—don't come near me." The voice was now unmistakably that of Stella Harold Spenser. "For God's sake, there's blood all over your hands. No—don't touch that *knife!*"

Four

IN THE STUDIO above the stable, Ellie lay back on the sofa, one hand over her eyes; she looked cheese-pale, bloodless, and her mouth was set in a firm hard line of self-control. John Lamb and Richard Owen Spenser stood staring at her, at the conundrum that she now represented.

Richie said, "I *know* we're right. It *has* to be Stella Bellfort. None of *my* family ordered those papers to be taken out of the library." His very emphasis revealed the depth of uncertainty that lay beneath the words.

Lamb went down on his knees by the sofa and put his arms around the tense, unyielding shoulders. Gently he said, "Ellie, darling—tell us exactly what happened, exactly how you felt and what you . . . you thought you saw."

Ellie would not answer. She turned a little away from him, leaning her cheek against the back of the sofa. When she dropped the hand from her eyes, Lamb saw once again, with a sinking of the heart, the blank withdrawn face of apathy which he had learned to know so well. He could almost feel her retreating from him, physically, as if she were walking away down a dark tunnel.

He stood up again and looked at her brother. "Okay," he said, "this is going to sound silly, but the whole

thing is a long way past reason. Is this place . . .
haunted or something?"

"I never heard any stories."

"The man who shot himself . . ."

"Not here. Miles away on a beach."

With one part of his mind Lamb was thinking that
this was absurd—two level-headed young men seri-
ously discussing whether the girl whom they both, in
different ways, loved was being haunted. Absurd! And
yet he had only spoken the truth when he had said that
the whole thing was now beyond reason.

Richie gestured. "Anyway, she lived here for six
months before she went to Europe, for Christ's sake!
There wasn't a thing the matter with her then."

Lamb looked back at Ellie. She had drawn up her
knees a little, and she had turned yet further away from
them. It was this attitude, this fetal attitude of the body
and a fetal absence of mind that went with it, which
worried and angered him the most. Up to this moment
he had fought that anger and contained it, but now,
suddenly, something beyond self-control took com-
mand of him: desperation perhaps, or plain fear, or
merely the amount of strong Greek wine he had taken
with his dinner. The anger broke out, surprising Richie
only a little more than it surprised himself.

He turned on the girl, kneeling over her on the sofa,
and gripped her hard by each tense shoulder; and he
began to shake her. "Ellie, will you *talk* to me. I love
you, remèmber? I'm the idiot who wants to spend the
rest of his life with you—I want to have babies with
you and look after you and *love* you, for God's sake—
so will you *talk to me?*"

Ellie tried to jerk away from him. She spoke as if

with some kind of impediment, shuddering. "Get away from me, get away from me—there's blood all over your hands!"

Self-control snapped. Lamb raised a hand and hit her hard across the face. Behind him Richie let out a gasp, took a pace forward, and checked himself.

John Lamb shouted, "You're going to *talk* to me, you're going to *look* at me, if I have to hit you until you're black and blue."

He was clearly—and to her brother's relief—not going to have to go that far. Perhaps a blow delivered in love has some built-in magic of its own, for Ellie had already looked up directly into the eyes of the young man she loved, and she now flung her arms around his neck, holding him close, gasping and choking, while he rocked her like a child. He was saying, "I'm sorry, I'm sorry," and she was saying, "What happened . . . Jesus, what happened, you hit me!"

Over her shoulder, Lamb said to Richie, "Coffee, I should think, wouldn't you? Lots of it, and pretty strong. And maybe a brandy too."

Richard left the coffee to percolate but returned more quickly with the brandy. Ellie, looking alive again, was sitting on the sofa while Lamb applied witch hazel to her left cheek. She said, "Yes, I do remember what I saw. I mean, I remember seeing it, but I don't remember anything after that until . . . until you socked me."

Lamb said, "Turn towards the light a little— Jesus, I don't know my own strength, do I? What did you see, what did you think you saw?"

"Blood. Really. That piece of wall just by the door there was . . . all smeared with it. Johnny, what's the *matter* with me?"

"That's what we're going to find out. At the moment, nothing."

She stared at him with a kind of bewildered trustfulness, like a child. Lamb said, "Well, obviously nothing —you can't see any blood there *now*, can you?"

"No, of course not—there isn't any."

"Okay. So now you're all right, aren't you? But you weren't all right then, and you did see it. What else?"

"On . . . on the doorknob. My God, I could *feel* it, how about that? I could actually feel that kind of . . . sticky feeling it has on my fingers."

"Yes, you kept looking at them. What else?"

Richard gave his sister a brandy, and she caught his hand as he withdrew it, holding him there. "You really are marvelous—both of you. What would I do without you?"

"With any luck," said Richie, "you won't *have* to do without either of us. Aren't you a lucky girl?"

John Lamb drank his brandy in one gulp, and choking a little, demanded, "What else?"

"I don't know. Or if I do . . ." She hesitated, and Lamb finished it for her: "If you do, it belongs to that . . . other place you go and live in from time to time."

Ellie nodded. "Is that how it seems?"

"Yes."

Richie, withdrawing his hand gently because he could hear the coffee making threatening noises, said, "What *is* that other place, Ell? What does it . . . feel like?"

"I don't know, that's just it."

Lamb said, "You come and go. One moment you're here and the next you're . . . somewhere else."

"Yes, I know. What I mean is . . . I guess I . . . kind of know when it's happening."

"Then why don't you fight it—resist it?"

"I do. Often I do, when you're here or . . . But when I'm by myself, or reading something that isn't really holding my interest . . ."

Richie said, "But what *happens*, Ellie—what does it actually feel like when it happens?"

Ellie thought for a time. "It's . . . Okay, this sounds crazy—it's like somebody . . . calling me." She shook her head. "I can't explain."

Amelia Guardi was saying, "But Lulu, I'm afraid you're going to *have* to explain. It's too important, it may even be vital."

Lulu Jenkins, now wearing her appalling pink-flannel dressing gown (she refused, for some reason, to part with it), lay slumped upon the pillows of her large bed, sipping Ovaltine and looking mutinous. Mrs. Guardi, as patiently determined as ever—only on this occasion, perhaps a shade more determined and a shade less patient—switched on the tape recorder. Lulu's voice, a little slurred as she gazed into the flame of the candle, said, "Tonight is . . . different." Amelia Guardi's voice said, "What do you mean, different?" For some time there was no sound but the whisper of the tape; then: "She, the girl, isn't there." Mrs. Guardi cut off her own voice saying, "Maybe that's better for us; it's Michael we must reach," because she knew that this was unessential and indeed mistaken. She said, "Lulu, the evening was . . . was a mess—incoherent. You yourself seemed to be . . . divided, uncertain. You've heard the tape; you must agree that it's quite different in tone, in *purpose,* from all the others.''

Lulu nodded, and sucked noisily at the last of her Ovaltine.

"Only when the young people came back from wherever they'd been did you . . . come to life, as it were. It's there on the tape, you can even hear the sound of the car.''

Lulu nodded again; then sighed deeply.

"Then, almost immediately, you mentioned the blood—and at the very same moment I heard Miss Owen Spenser scream. I ran straight to the window overlooking the yard—and what did I see? She was in a state of shock—almost fainting, I would say—and she was crying out about blood, about having seen blood.''

The sigh which Lulu Jenkins now heaved up from the recesses of her big body was definitive; she peered hopefully into her mug, but it was indeed empty.

"So—am I correct in deducing that when you said, 'She, the girl, isn't there,' you didn't mean, as I thought, Catherine or Leona or any of the others connected with the past—you meant Ellie Owen Spenser.''

Silence.

"Lulu, am I correct?''

At long last, "Yes. I wasn't sure. I thought that perhaps . . . She has perception—extraordinary perception.''

"In fact, she's psychic, a contact?''

"No. It has to do . . . with this house. Sometimes I find . . .'' She spread both her fat hands in one of her rare purely Gallic gestures. "I find that I am . . . There are no words for these things, a new dictionary is needed. I find I am inside her mind.''

Amelia Guardi nodded, her strange secretive eyes fixed on the other woman's face; at these moments she was sure that given a "new dictionary," Lulu Jenkins could indeed surprise the world. "And what do you . . . see inside her mind?"

"She is greatly troubled."

"She's in love."

"Yes, that troubles her. And there are other things connected with it; she's afraid of having children, I'm not sure why . . ." The voice faded; the pale eyes were half closed. Was she at this very instant, Amelia Guardi wondered, inside the mind of Ellie Owen Spenser?

Lulu sighed again, deeply. "She loves him very much . . . and . . . I don't know. Hereditary perhaps."

"Hereditary? What?" Very sharp.

But she was to receive no answer. After a time Lulu said, "Yes, when she is here, *they* are very close. When she is away . . . Things proceed normally when she is away, but when she is here it is all very . . . distinct. Something in her—in her psyche—is linked to that poor, poor woman . . ."

"Stella?"

"Yes."

Mrs. Guardi went and sat on the bed so that she could see the other woman's face quite clearly. She said, "Lulu, my dear, are you telling me that because of some . . . shared emotional experience, the girl, Ellie, is linked through time with Stella Harold Spenser."

"These things are never definite . . ."

"But crudely, in essentials, you think that is the case?"

"Yes." Unhappily.

"Both love a man—and the two men, for different

reasons, are a source of deep worry, of unhappiness, to them."

"Yes." The fat fingers had begun to pluck at the quilt in agitation. "I don't like it. And it may . . . It may not be good for the girl; we have so little true knowledge of such things."

"If," said Amelia Guardi, ignoring these last observations, "if she is close to Stella, then she is also close to the man she loved—to this Michael?"

"Yes, there are times . . ." She shook her head, frowning.

"Times?"

"When the two men become . . . confused in her mind. I think there are times when he, this Mikey, is very close to her. Perhaps too close."

"Too close?"

"He was not a good man. And the woman, Stella . . . There is something to fear in her too."

Mrs. Guardi stood up from the bed and began to prowl about the room. Lulu watched her unhappily. "You see," she said, almost pleading, "it may be bad for the girl; there is no way of telling how it may affect her."

In a hard voice which Lulu had not heard before— and which she ought to have found very revealing, except for the fact that human relationships had left no mark of experience on her extraordinary mind— Amelia Guardi said, "The young and strong are not affected by such things." She turned swiftly, excitedly back to the bed. "But for us it's an unbelievable stroke of luck. We must use it, Lulu, we must use it to the full."

"I don't want to be responsible . . ."

"Don't worry. I'll visit the girl from time to time—make sure she's all right. I'll . . . Oh, there are a dozen ways we can check on her." She sat down again and took one of the plump agitated hands between both her own. "It would be criminal, Lulu, to miss an opportunity like that."

"You don't seem to understand the kind of dangers . . . We walk in an unknown land."

"It's our mission, Lulu—our great and splendid mission—to be the first explorers in that land. Nothing must stand in our way, *nothing.*"

Lulu Jenkins gazed at her mournfully.

"When our work is published—when we reveal all that we have discovered in that new world—everything will be justified, everything forgiven." She saw that the old magic was beginning to do its work somewhere behind the pale-green stare. "Do you imagine that Livingstone would have hesitated? Could a man like . . . like Pasteur allow little considerations to stand in his way? No. And neither will we." She patted the fat, helpless hand. "The girl will come to no harm. Let that be my problem—you mustn't worry your head about such things."

She could see that once again the seed, so carefully planted, so tender, so carefully nurtured, was sprouting afresh. The green eyes were even looking quite intelligent for once. It was clearly the moment to disappear—which she did, after planting a comforting goodnight kiss on the plump cheek—leaving Lulu to dwell upon dreams of glory.

But in fact this was one of the very few times when Amelia Guardi had ever underestimated her recalcitrant camel. The glow of intelligence in Lulu's odd eyes had not been induced by the usual dream of glory, but by the far more unusual (for Lulu) fact of memory.

In Claridge's, at some point during or after that magnificent tea—there had been a very good walnut cake, she now recalled—she had said, "I don't see how we shall begin our . . . work." And Mrs. Guardi had said, "That's my problem, my dear. You mustn't worry your head about such things." At that time Lulu Jenkins had experienced no more than a vague feeling of disquiet; but this time ("The girl will come to no harm. Let that be my problem—you mustn't worry your head about such things") memory had reincarnated for her, alive and whole and nauseating, Jolly Jackie Jenkins himself. He was standing in front of the long mirror in their rented house in Chelsea, London, S.W.3.; he was carefully tying the knot of a repulsive yellow and brown tie, and he was saying, "It's only for a couple of nights, my old darling, don't get in a fret."

So then Lulu had said, "But why Birmingham? I don't see there's anything for us in Birmingham—or anywhere else until I'm . . . well again."

"You leave that to me," replied Jolly Jackie, putting on his coat and picking up his overnight bag, which, had she tried to lift it, she would have found suspiciously heavy. "That's my problem, girlie—you mustn't worry your head about such things." And then, with a kiss on the cheek, he had walked out of the room, out of the house, and out of the life of Lulu Jenkins forever, taking with him all the money which she had earned for him.

It would be a mistake to suppose that Lulu had suddenly begun to mistrust Amelia Guardi because she had, by chance, used the phrase with which Jackie Jenkins had betrayed his stodgy and no-longer-useful wife; even Lulu's odd mind did not work on quite so superficial an everyday level. In any case, many things about Mrs. Guardi had seemed to her disquieting right from the start. Nothing definite. In Lulu's mind nothing was ever definite because it was operating on so many different levels at the same time. If she had been able to analyze things, which, perhaps mercifully, was a total impossibility, she would have found that her impressions of a person were an extraordinary amalgam of their psychic persona (sometimes called an "aura"), their birth date, the numerological indications of their full name, their actual physical smell, their eyes, the way they used their hands, the shape of their fingernails, the sound of their voice (rather than the actual things they said), the reaction to them of animals, if there happened to be any animals around, and another six or seven aspects of them which would probably defy not only analysis but the words available to man for the purposes of communicating that analysis.

Lulu had only actually seen Ellie, with her eyes, three times from a window, briefly; but she knew her quite well—better, possibly, than an average person ever gets to "know" a friend, lover, or spouse. She liked what she knew, and as she lay in her large bed, staring at the wall and remembering Jolly Jackie Jenkins, a rare and positive practical thought wavered into her mind. She was in the habit of dismissing positive and practical thoughts because she knew from experience that they tended to lead to positive and practical action, and any such action she had ever taken had turned out to be disastrous. The thought, resolutely refusing to be dismissed, was that in some way it was her duty to warn Ellie of the danger to which Amelia Guardi seemed prepared, and even determined, to expose her.

Part III

THE
DEAD

One

ROBERT HILLIER took the thick envelope, containing the fourteen Spenser case histories, out of the
safe-deposit box with a sinking heart. If he had eaten
them all for breakfast, their weight could not have lain
so heavily on his stomach as it did now.

He took them to his consulting room on Sutter
Street, knowing that since this was not one of his
official days there, he would be left in peace. He sat
down at the desk and slit open the envelope. Inside it
were two others, a circumstance which surprised him
until he had examined them, whereupon they revealed
themselves as being yet another facet of his father-in-
law's tidy mind. On both of them was written a list of
names—the names of the case histories which they
contained. Why divide them? The answer became
painfully obvious.

On the fatter envelope were listed: William, son of
the famous or infamous "Old Dick" who had struck
gold down in Nevada; then his two daughters, Elizabeth Maud and Sarah Rose (whose diaries had been
inspected by John Lamb and Richie at the Lilienthal
Library); then Owen, his son, who had gone away to
Philadelphia following the great family row. There was
also the name of Owen's wife, Mary, and those of their
three children: Rose, who had married an English

baronet; Edward, who had become a priest; and Charles, who had fathered Ellie and Richard. Eight people in all—it seemed that Charles's wife, Josephine Acland from Boston, had preferred her own physician.

In the second envelope, Robert Hillier understood even before he looked at the names, were the case histories of the Harold Spenser side of the family; the fact that old Dr. Macfadden had divided them so neatly caused his stomach to drop yet further. He knew exactly what was coming; hadn't he been avoiding it for two weeks—perhaps longer, perhaps for years? Yes, there they were: Harold himself, and his wife Stella (born Bellfort), and their five children, Hugh, Catherine, Leona, Patrick and Matthew—for even if Hugh had occasionally consulted his old friend from Harvard, it seemed that he had not been able to resist the wisdom and kindliness of the old Scotsman as well.

Robert Hillier knew that there might be things he would want to check concerning the Owen Spensers, in order to set his mind at rest (would it ever be at rest again?) about Ellie, but it was the Harold Spenser envelope which he now opened. A sheet of his father-in-law's blue notepaper fell out on top of the neatly typed folders.

These case histories were removed from my file at the request of Godfrey Bellfort, brother of Stella Harold Spenser. Legally they are my property, willed to you, Robert, with all my other medical effects. But in view of the enormous wealth and influence of the Bellfort family, I urge you to be careful of the use to which you put them.

Robert Hillier sighed. So here it was, the hard

unemotional truth, background to a whole Apocrypha
of gossip which still echoed on across the years in the
wake of the strange, exciting, and exotic (weren't those
the adjectives his wife had used?) Harold Spensers. It
was like encountering a dream, many dreams, on
waking; so much that was here he already knew,
without knowing quite when or how he had heard it.

In April 1919, ". . . it was Owen, still in uniform,
who made the appointment, saying that he hoped to be
able to bring Harold to see me. I knew that already they
were hardly on speaking terms, though I was unaware
of the reason . . .

". . . soon made it clear. Harold was at his most
obstinate, Owen at his most outspoken. He demanded
that I forbid his brother to marry the girl. I had to
remind him that everything he had said was based
solely on hearsay; famous and rich families are always
talked about; the Bellforts were as much on the
tongues of every gossip as were the Spensers themselves.

". . . adding that I was merely a physician, not God;
I was in no position to forbid anything, least of all a
marriage between two young people who were so very
much in love. Owen said that if a patient had bronchitis
I would certainly stop him going to a football match on
a very cold day . . .

"It was impossible to make Owen understand (or
rather admit that he could understand) my position as
a doctor. I had never held professional consultation
with any member of the Bellfort family. Moreover, Dr.
Hymes, who was their physician, was not only no
friend of mine and a pigheaded old man to boot, but
could claim with absolute integrity that he had no right

to disclose any private details concerning the Bellforts.

". . . not in my power to be more helpful in my capacity as their doctor; but I did urge Harold to be bold and to tackle the subject directly—with his proposed father-in-law if he dared, and/or depending on circumstances, with young Godfrey Bellfort, Stella's brother, if that seemed more advisable.

"In fact—or so Harold told me—he talked to both men, who pooh-poohed the whole idea, dismissing it as malicious gossip. Harold was satisfied that there was not, and never had been, any taint of insanity in the Bellfort family. As for Owen . . .

". . . never spoke to me or to his brother again . . . Philadelphia . . ."

Harold Spenser and Stella Bellfort were married on September 16, 1919.

Robert Hillier skipped several pages, his eye running professionally over the ordinary and minor ailments which had afflicted Harold Spenser from time to time. Then he picked up the next folder: Stella Bellfort Harold Spenser.

The first notes showed admiration for the splendid physical health of the young bride. No fears of any kind when she became pregnant, "a most sensible and practical expectant mother." Hugh had been born at five A.M. on June 29, 1920—an easy birth, a fine boy. Hillier's eye ran cursorily over a bad chest cold, a possible fear of pleurisy, in December 1920, and noted that at the time Stella was again pregnant. There was a quick recovery, followed by a Merry Christmas. Catherine had been born on August 3, 1921. Stella, it seemed, had been subject to certain hysterical fears regarding the birth.

"In view of the ease of Hugh's delivery, and her desire to have another child as quickly as possible, I find this a little surprising, though a not unusual psychological aspect of pregnancy." Against this comment, the old doctor had penciled (at what time, after what events?) a question mark.

In fact, the labor, this time, had been protracted and painful. Neither this nor the "hysterical fears" could have had any lasting effect, for Leona had been born in June of 1923, and Patrick a little less than two years later, in April 1925. Between the two births came the first of the dark signs, a puzzled entry which had been annotated later in pencil: ". . . a perfectly ordinary case of mild hysteria. The trigger, however, hardly seems reason enough for her state of mind—namely, the fact that her husband had been forced to spend an extra day and night in Chicago, where his board meeting had been more complicated than at first expected." The penciled note, wise after the event, was bleak: "First signs of autistic behavior?" Under this was a note: "AUTISM—finding pleasure in fantasies that represent reality in wish-fulfilling terms, even when these are not believed."

Dr. Hillier sighed to himself.

In March 1926, when her husband had again been away on business, the police had called Dr. Macfadden. "I assured her that it was entirely impossible for a man to even reach the window in question, let alone hang there for a long period, looking in. The whole incident was pure fantasy, resulting perhaps from some half-waking dream. She seemed quite satisfied . . . Sedative . . ."

Stella may have been satisfied; evidently her husband was not. The visit was cross-referenced and recorded in his file, not hers. "It seemed to me that he was making too much fuss if the two incidents I knew of were all there was to it. I asked him whether he, in the privacy of their relationship, had experienced others of which he had not told me . . .

"We have been friends a long time, and I must say that his unwillingness to discuss this situation struck me with foreboding . . . for such an outspoken man . . . indeed, it was the nearest we ever got to a real quarrel."

Harold Spenser was perhaps remembering that scene with his brother—was remembering, with regret possibly, that his brother had put a continent, and a barrier of impenetrable silence, between the two of them. That day—in March 1926—he had stormed out of the doctor's consulting room in a fury. A week later he was back. The night before, it seemed, while he himself was in the bathroom next door, a man had broken into Stella's bedroom and exposed himself to her. Why hadn't she called out? She had, but the noise of the shower had drowned her voice! Harold Spenser's defenses were down. "He implored me, no matter what the cost, to call in whatever assistance I required—to investigate the causes of this childish storytelling and to get rid of it." The whole sinister avalanche had shown its flaw and was beginning to move—at first so slowly that the human eye could hardly measure the movement. For Stella had admitted that she was drinking a little too much—had admitted that, tipsy, she had been teasing Harold. And Harold himself had admitted that pressure of work and concomitant weariness *had* been curtailing their sexual relationship. The resumption of this, it seemed, had put a temporary end to Stella's problems!

Robert Hillier sighed again. How naïve they seemed, the psychological pronouncements of that time—less than fifty years ago! Presumably the old doctor had thought them naïve himself, when he came to read them again later—but by then Harold Spenser had revealed that from the first his wife had made sexual demands which he found it difficult to satisfy. "Was she always," the note in the margin asked, "obsessed by sex?"

In May of 1927 Stella was at it again. A man had stopped her car, asking for a lift; he had exposed himself to her. The police of any city cannot allow such things to happen to the wife of a leading citizen; yet there was now, in Dr. Macfadden's description of the incident, a hint of conspiratorial understanding between the doctor and the law.

By September of that year she was again pregnant. Hugh was now seven years old, Catherine six, Leona four, and Patrick two. Stella suddenly claimed that the father of the expected child was not her husband, but a man who had taken advantage of her in a train. At the time she had been traveling with Elizabeth Maud, her sister-in-law; she had not been out of Elizabeth Maud's sight for more than five minutes during the entire journey . . . But what did actual reason matter now?

The penciled note in the margin read: "PARANOID SCHIZOPHRENIA: unrealistic thinking, hallucinations, and many often highly elaborate and systemized delusions, particularly of persecution or grandeur. The whole personality is affected, and there is likely to be deterioration . . ."

The avalanche was beginning to move more quickly. Moreover, its flaw was now seen to be manifold; dangerous cracks ran beneath the surface in all directions. At Christmas four-year-old Leona was seized by some mysterious ailment which was at first taken to be flu, since there was a bad epidemic that year. However, no fever developed and no virus could be located. Specialists were sent for from as far away as Vienna. Dr. Macfadden had cross-referenced the incident in the father's file as well as in the child's. Harold Spenser was in such a state that the doctor had "prescribed not only a barbiturate at night, but a mild sedative to be taken three times during the day. He spoke openly to me of Owen, and the terrible arguments which had finally put an end to their close relationship. He wanted to send for Owen, and I encouraged him to do so, but pride was stronger than reason. After all, he said, there might be a simple way out of the nightmare."

There was no way out. Leona's file described in detail the efforts made by several distinguished doctors to find one. "The entire nervous system," one note pointed out, "seems to be unbalanced." Then there was a reversal; the little girl seemed "cured"; she had always been overexcitable and nervous—character traits which had once appeared rather ordinary but which now struck the family doctor with disquiet. He was right. A month later Leona announced that she had seen Jesus in a vision and that when she grew up she was going to be a nun; at fourteen this might have been a normal phase, at four it seemed unlikely; the child began to talk about Jesus continually. The penciled quotation read, "In most forms of schizophrenia, excessive religiosity may be present."

The avalanche was in full fall, gathering up whatever lay in its path. On May 13, 1928, this particular avalanche (by no means the last and by no means the worst) hit the valley floor; Stella Harold Spenser's fifth child, Matthew, was born at eight o'clock in the morning.

"I had, as usual, called in Dr. Griffiths. The conclusion was, we both felt, foregone, but we saw it as our duty to consult other opinion. Dr. Weibach and Dr. Holmes both agreed one hundred percent with our analysis . . .

"The head was perhaps three times normal size, and the body disproportionately undersized. The sex, though not indeterminate, would not in the opinion of all of us have developed to any degree, owing to . . .

"The mother was therefore kept under sedation."

Hillier stood up and began to pace around the consulting room; he took some Kleenex from a box and wiped away the dew of sweat which was trickling down his forehead. So the mother had been kept under sedation, but there was none for the wretched father; no peace and no rest until he prescribed them both for himself with a bullet.

There was an echo of his anguish even in the old doctor's conscientiously unemotional notes, and undoubtedly his own integrity had been put to a severe test. The specialists had now agreed that Leona would never be entirely normal. Patrick was a sickly boy, exhibiting as he grew older something less than average intelligence. Catherine, aged seven, was certainly intelligent but she had been caught out in three strange misdemeanors involving cruelty, which were hard to explain within the terms of reference applicable to a normal child—two involving a puppy and one involving her baby brother. (Hugh, aged eight, seemed to be the exception, a fat and unimaginative child doing mildly well at a private school in the East.) Now there was Matthew, quite simply a monster, and overall there was Stella—paranoid schizophrenia: "The whole personality is affected, and there is likely to be deterioration."

Humankind is very good at making judgments—less good at coping with its own problems. We all deal with the impossible as best we may—Harold Spenser went out on a lonely beach and shot himself. Stella was too ill to attend the funeral. Owen crossed the continent to be present; he was visibly much moved; nobody (not even Dr. Macfadden) could guess how much of the truth he knew, but in any case, there is no consolation in being right.

Alas, it was not the end; it was a long, long way from being the end. Robert Hillier lit a cigarette and sat down at his desk again. In view of the action which he was pretty sure he was going to have to take, he was interested in a note which his father-in-law had added at the end of Harold Spenser's file—under the neatly ruled line which seemed almost to be a visible symbol of his death. It was headed "The Bellforts," and though short, was crisply to the point, very typical of the man who had written it.

"As family physician to the Harold Spensers, Stella in particular, I considered it my duty to approach Godfrey Bellfort after the funeral. Though seven years younger than Stella, he is now head of the family, following his father's death in an air crash in the winter of '24; he is twenty-nine, but has been trained all his life (as the only son of a great fortune) to take over the reins. I can't say that I liked him, but I was forced to admire the strength of his character.

"I told him, openly and honestly, that the mental condition of all his sister's children, with the exception of Hugh, left a good deal to be desired; I told him most of what poor Harold had told me about his wife's idiosyncrasies, and I told him that I knew the reason for Harold and Owen Spenser's estrangement had been the suitability of Stella as a wife and mother.

"I'm not sure what answer I expected, but now that I know Godfrey Bellfort a little better, I realize that the one I got was a foregone conclusion. There was no taint of insanity in the Bellfort family, none whatever. If Stella's children were abnormal in any way, the fault lay in Spenser blood, and indeed he himself had always been against his sister marrying into that family.

"I think, even then, he knew this to be a reversal of the truth, but it was the line he had decided to take, and it was the line (he let me know very directly) that he expected me to take also. He even went so far as to threaten me—I can use no other word—with the power and wealth of the Bellforts, intimating that any thoughtless remarks on my part would lead to a court-of-law and/or the loss of my practice in an area where all my richest patients were old friends of his family.

"I replied, with what dignity I could muster (which wasn't much), that I was first and foremost a doctor, and as such, sworn to keep the private concerns of my patients strictly private. By this time I think he had come to have *some* regard for my character and integrity, though it is never his way to reveal such 'weakness,' and he thanked me for having been a good friend to his sister; he managed, in the same breath, to imply that I was in love with her, but obviously to him this was quite normal.

"I cannot say that we parted with any degree of mutual partiality, but at least the situation between us was crystal-clear. If I behaved myself vis-à-vis the Bellforts, I could look forward to a healthy, successful, and prosperous life. If I didn't, God help me."

A penciled note under these half-dozen revealing paragraphs read, "Twenty-five years later I find that I have nothing to add to this description of Bellfort. Age has only polished the steel of that character. He is ruthless, selfish, apparently without human failing or feeling—yet he is more than the sum of these things, and, most extraordinary of all, though one could never like him, it is impossible to *dis*like him—he is so complete."

Robert Hillier sat back in his chair and considered this description through a haze of cigarette smoke. It seemed to him inevitable that sooner or later, and probably sooner, he was going to have to acquaint Bellfort with Ellie's condition—or rather, the reactions to it of John Lamb, that dogged lover, and Richard Owen Spenser, that vitriolic brother and pederast. Dimly he could even foresee a meeting between these parties with himself in attendance; he didn't know whether he was more curious or anxious as to the outcome. He returned to the files.

Immediately following Harold's suicide and the merciful death of the pathetic bundle of skin and bone that had briefly borne the name of Matthew, Stella had been taken away by her brother to the fastness of his ranch in Colorado; the children went too. Following the "accidental" wounding of a newspaperman by one of the estate guards, the press decided to give Mrs. Harold Spenser a rest from publicity. It was well over a year before Dr. Macfadden saw any of them again.

In May 1930 Stella came back to San Francisco with Hugh, Catherine, and little Patrick, aged ten, nine, and five, respectively. It was understood that Leona had stayed with her Uncle Godfrey in Colorado, but Stella told her old friend and doctor the truth. He had drawn a line under the few entries that made up her case history; it did not, as in her father's case, mean death, but might just as well have done so; Leona had been admitted to the first of a long series of "sanatoria," where she would spend the next forty years of her wasted life.

Robert Hillier turned to Patrick's file. As he had suspected, the little boy was only going to live two years longer. "At seven years and two months," Dr. Macfadden had written, "he displayed only the most rudimentary intelligence and could be extremely destructive." Maybe the pneumonia which ruled the line across *his* case history was merciful. The old doctor had certainly considered it so.

That left Hugh and Catherine, both of them at school. With no husband and no children at hand, and far too much money demanding to be spent, it was hardly surprising that Stella Harold Spenser slid, almost without realizing it, into that period of her life which had given the gossips so much delicious sustenance.

In 1932 she was thirty-nine years old, an aging but still very beautiful woman, well preserved and more than a little interested in sex—as her dead husband had once admitted to Dr. Macfadden. The first scandal broke less than a year later; it involved the chauffeur of a socially and financially prominent family, and it was followed by what the newspapers described as a "nervous breakdown." This was to become the pattern, a pattern with which the old doctor was going to become all too well acquainted.

"She is exhausted, totally without energy, exhibiting a slight fever, a slowed pulse rate and periodic bouts of childish bad temper which exhaust her even more. I told her plainly that I was not equipped to do more than handle the physical aspect of her condition, and that I would be happy to call in a good psychiatrist. This produced another outburst of temper, followed by tears. It is quite clear that her entire nervous system is off balance; she veers from extreme to extreme, and I doubt if she is at any time in an entirely 'normal' condition."

The good friend also suggested, as tactfully as possible, that if she was going to amuse herself with young men, it would be better to choose anonymous ones— better still, to go and do it in some other place where she was less well known. Stella, it seemed, laughed. She had entered into a relationship with her doctor which now went beyond the usual bounds; "my father confessor," she once called him, and this was what he became. Her case history listed all that she told him, but he took to putting in parentheses those stories which seemed to him to be pure fabrication. He did not like the situation, but . . . "It seems to me that if I don't play this game with her, somebody else will: somebody who is not her friend and who will certainly, one way or another, make capital out of it."

So he played the part of "father confessor" but he couldn't also take the part of lover; and the next young man showed every promise of being much more dangerous than the chauffeur—so dangerous that Dr. Macfadden had summoned Godfrey Bellfort.

Typically, Bellfort listened to every word the doctor had to say, and made no answer of any kind. He merely said, "Thank you," went to Number 337 Gilman Street, and locked himself in with his sister. The young man in question left San Francisco next morning; Stella left three days later with her brother, bound for Europe. It was Bellfort who paid Dr. Macfadden's outstanding account: $276 for professional services, and $10,000 for services not specified. Enraged, the doctor had sent the latter to his favorite children's hospital, forwarding their receipt to Godfrey Bellfort. He did not see Stella Harold Spenser again for two years, but like the rest of socially acceptable San Francisco, he was kept well informed of her career. Never a neighbor returned from Paris, from Rome, from Monte Carlo, Vienna, or Biarritz without a succulent tidbit for the wide-open mouths on Pacific Heights. Gondoliers, ski instructors, hotel porters, beachboys, tennis pros—no cliché, it seemed, was too outworn for the ex-Mrs. Harold Spenser. When the news came hot from the Via Veneto that she had actually got married, the general opinion was "Well, this one has to be *something!*"

And something was what Michael Burke turned out to be.

● ● ●

Robert Hillier remembered that his own wife had said that he was the most *gorgeous* man—that they were all in love with him. He also remembered, from some ancient piece of gossip, that there had been doubts as to the young man's actual origin; he had been entitled to British nationality, but in those days before World War II this could have meant almost anything, and in Burke's case, probably did.

"I have often noticed," Dr. Macfadden had written, "that certain people of either sex sometimes project a sensual appeal which is not directly connected with sexual attraction. Within our knowledge of that tired word 'normal' as applied to sexual preference, this sensual projection may be felt by a normal man for another, or by a normal woman for another. It is very beguiling; it is innocent, though the one who projects it may be the least innocent person alive. Stella's young husband, Michael Burke, possesses it to a quite remarkable degree. He is also, I think, a rogue and a fortune hunter. The mixture may well prove dangerous."

Robert Hillier grimaced to himself. His father-in-law had just met the young man in question for the first time; an ankle, originally injured while skiing, had succumbed to the hills of San Francisco.

Stella, it seemed, was "looking better than she has looked since Harold's death; she has put on a little weight and the blood pressure is back to normal. The pulse is a little fast, but I tell her there is nothing to worry about." The old doctor did not at this point mention any of the things he himself must have been worrying about; it almost seemed as if he was trying not to tempt providence, and knowing him well, Hillier was sure that he would not wish to add anything to the tide of surmise and doubt which was at that time sweeping through the drawing rooms of what might be called "*tout* San Francisco." His only comment lay in a single exclamation mark at the top of the new case sheet he had started for Mr. Burke. It followed his age: Twenty-four! Stella was now forty-three. Hugh (sixteen) and Catherine (fifteen) came back to San Francisco for the vacation, and to meet their stepfather. It was a pity, Hillier thought, that their opinions of him were not quoted; but Dr. Macfadden's opinion of *them* was, when, as a matter of course, they visited the family physician for a vacation checkup: "Hugh is like his father physically; he will be a big man; in the classroom, apparently, he plods along steadily enough, but on the football field he is something of a star. This is a good thing; for one reason and another both Harold Spenser children need all the self-esteem they can muster. Their father's way of death, not to mention their mother's way of life—not to mention the unmentioned presence of Leona in the background—require some compensation."

At Stella's request, Dr. Macfadden had broached the subject of sex with her son. "He seems quite sophisticated about it, has 'done it once' with a girl after a prom, and does not approve of masturbation because 'it affects your game'—football, of course."

Catherine was evidently less straightforward. "Menstruation started at thirteen; she has therefore been a woman for two years and some months. She is well developed, with something of her mother's excellent figure, but, alas, none of her mother's charm . . ." The good old doctor's feeling about the girl wavered with uncharacteristic indecision; at times he was sorry for her: "She is very aware of the fate of her younger brothers. She remembers Patrick well and perhaps misses him; she is curious about Matthew, who, she has been told, was dead at birth; she is interested in Leona but evades the issue in a strange way, which is perhaps natural." At other times his patience obviously ran out: "It seems a terrible thing to say of a child of this age, but I cannot like her; she is slippery and too evasive; sometimes I think she is laughing at all of us. Though it seems absurd, I must in honesty record that I do not like physical contact with her; I should add that no other patient, male or female, has affected me in quite this way."

As for Stella, it was impossible to say from the case histories just when the trouble began all over again. She had a great regard for her old friend and doctor, and possibly did not want to demean herself in his eyes by admitting that, so soon, her new marriage was coming apart at the seams. What he guessed he kept to himself; the case histories, so near to his heart, were founded only on fact and observation, not on guess-work. It was not until mid-1937, a warm July, that she called him suddenly in the small hours of the morning. He was appalled, but not surprised, by what he found.

". . . an advanced state of hysteria. She has lost too much weight, is smoking and drinking too much and, not wishing to involve me, has been to Dr.—— who prescribed barbitumene-A, of which I don't approve. She had, she told me, taken three tablets on top of a good deal of Scotch. Somewhat naturally, her heart-beat was most irregular, and this had scared her into sending for me . . .

"In fact, as I had foreseen as soon as I heard her voice on the phone, the disorder is psychological. The marriage is a farce; Burke was not even in the house (at three A.M.), but had called to say that he was involved in a poker game. He is, apparently, involved in 'poker games' almost every night.

"She begged me not to speak to him, and revealed that he has never liked the intimacy of her association with me. Hardly surprising! She also begged me not on any account to appeal to her brother, who was against the marriage from the start. Again, hardly surprising . . .

". . . begged me to stay with her; she said she felt that Harold was angry with her, and that if she was left alone, she was afraid that she too might commit suicide.

"Somewhere in all this there is a tremendous sense of guilt; did she in fact know, at the time she married Harold, that there was mental instability in her family? If so, poor woman, she feels that she is paying for it now. I don't think it is for me to inquire into this, and I cannot now see myself continuing to treat her without the help of a specially qualified doctor . . .

"As was to be expected, Burke returned while I was still with her. I wished to speak to him at once but was deterred (a) by her terror of my doing so, (b) by my own fear that in doing so I might make matters worse between them, and (c) because he was very drunk.

"I was now put in the ridiculous position of being locked into her room while she shouted at him to go away from her—to sleep on his own. It was not long before he was snoring in the room across the hall. By five-thirty A.M. I judged that her heart was in a condition, which permitted me to give her an injection of dethodril. She was asleep in ten minutes, and I was free to return home.

"Obviously, I can't allow this to continue, and I cannot be responsible, alone, for what happens to this unfortunate woman. The situation can only deteriorate."

But he did remain responsible and alone, and the situation did deteriorate. Hillier knew, because the older man had told him, that even normally placid Mrs. Macfadden had become involved—resenting, perhaps naturally, the number of times that her husband was summoned from his bed to minister to the hysterical woman at 337 Gilman Street—resenting also the rumors which had begun to circulate concerning the relationship between her husband and his patient. By October 1937 the strain was beginning to tell on the doctor himself, as a string of petty illnesses proved. He made up his mind to ignore Stella's wishes, to talk to Michael Burke, and, if necessary, to summon Godfrey Bellfort.

Burke was "mocking and abusive." "He told me that it was common knowledge that I had always been in love with his wife, and that for this reason he does not consider me competent to be her doctor. As for their 'troubles,' they are none of my business; all married couples have them, and there is nothing about them that cannot be solved between husband and wife.

"Of course, in spite of my asking him not to, he told Stella that I had spoken to him. She was furious with me and now won't even see me. If all this has in any way mended their relationship, I don't in the least mind playing my new part of Wicked Old Doctor, but I fear that the respite will only be temporary. He is young, hot-blooded, very attractive, and possessed of that fatal charm; also, he drinks too much. A woman of forty-four cannot possibly satisfy a young man of this type, nineteen years her junior."

Whatever the reason, there was an uneasy lull in the battle, and Dr. Macfadden had not thought it necessary to appeal to Godfrey Bellfort; perhaps the mere sound of that name had been enough to bring the young man to heel. He bought his wife a number of expensive gifts with her own money, including a fabulous piece of Fabergé, and they took a trip to Mexico. Catherine and Hugh joined them there for Christmas.

With their return the final chapter opened. As far as Dr. Macfadden was concerned, it opened with a bang. He called at Gilman Street to see Stella, who had been suffering from the usual upset stomach which inflicts itself on every traveler in Mexico, however wary, and "walked into the most horrifying row between parent and child that it has ever been my experience to witness." Catherine and her mother were at it "like a couple of fishwives," and the noise, even some of the words, could be heard up and down the street. Later he wrote, "It is strange for a doctor to have to admit fear; we see and hear a good deal, and few things frighten us; but there was a malevolence loose in that house that afternoon which rooted me to the bottom of the staircase.

"I do not wish to quote any of the phrases used—they should never have been uttered, either by the woman or the child (in fact, I can't imagine where Catherine learned them in the first place)—but it seemed clear that Stella had caught her, more than once, listening behind doors and also peeping . . ." He had added in retrospect, "This was a little naïve of me. If the girl had a habit of listening behind doors, there is practically no word she could not have learned from the slanging-matches between her mother and her young stepfather, particularly when both had been drinking."

He noted that Stella's physical condition had deteriorated alarmingly. "She was literally a bundle of nerves held together by skin and bone. I told her that I would no longer take no for an answer; she must see a specialist immediately. She refused, and said that if 'one of those brainwashers' came to the door, he would not be allowed in.

"Twice during the conversation she shouted towards the door, telling Catherine to go away. On each occasion I checked; the girl was not there. During all this I could not banish the sensation in the pit of the stomach which I must call 'fear.' She was exhibiting so violent a nervous tension that I offered to give her an injection to alleviate it; she refused this also, saying that she must stay awake—there was no telling what would happen if she slept. Clearly the delusions of persecution had moved into a new phase (see PARANOID SCHIZOPHRENIA), and had turned on her young husband and her daughter . . .

"As soon as I got home I called the Bellfort offices downtown. They told me that Godfrey Bellfort was in Zurich on business; I said that it was vitally urgent that I speak to him, and they promised to relay the message at once. (His telephone numbers are never given to outsiders.)

"He called me late the same night—from Rome. I told him that I was very worried about his sister's condition—that she had refused to see any other doctor, and that I myself could no longer be held responsible for her. I don't know what his feelings were; he simply said, 'Do you consider it necessary for me to come to San Francisco?' I replied in the affirmative. He said he would leave immediately, using his own plane. He asked me to go to Stella and stay with her, all the time, if necessary, until he arrived; he would see to it that my loyalty was well repaid.

"I went back to 337 Gilman Street right away. A manservant refused to admit me, saying that Mrs. Burke did not wish to see anybody. I thought that this might be some trick of her husband's, but as I went back to my car I chanced to look up at the house; she was standing at the window of the first-floor library, watching me go. Seeing her, I hesitated, but as soon as I did so, she shook her head and moved out of sight. I never saw her again."

This was on April 3, 1938. Dr. Macfadden, the good friend, had gone back next day only to be met by the same manservant with the same message. On the morning of the fifth, as he again approached the house, he saw Catherine going in at the front door. Nobody answered his ring. On the sixth he received a note from Godfrey Bellfort, written on 337 Gilman Street paper: it said that Dr. Macfadden was not to worry; everything was now under control; if his services were required, Bellfort himself would send for him, but this seemed unlikely. After that there was silence. Whatever was going on in the big house, San Francisco knew nothing of it and neither did Dr. Macfadden or any of his colleagues.

On April 8, amid a glitter of illustrious names—Mr. Lewis Luckenback, Mrs. Elizabeth Sprague Coolidge, Mrs. Thomas Page Maillard, et al.—there appeared in that well-known column "Cholly's Notebook" the following paragraph: "Off to Europe yet again, that handsome couple Mr. and Mrs. Michael Burke. (She, of course, was our own glamorous Stella Harold Spenser for all those years.) They will visit Paris, London, Madrid, and Rome, and plan to be away several months."

Later that month Godfrey Bellfort again paid Dr. Macfadden's outstanding account. This time he did not include a $10,000 tip; perhaps he didn't like to waste his money on children's hospitals. It was understood that Catherine had been sent to boarding school in the East, in order to be near her brother, Hugh, and her Aunt Violet, with whom she would spend the vacations when she was not visiting her mother and stepfather in Europe.

Stella Harold Spenser/Burke's case history ended with three more press cuttings and a note in the old doctor's neat handwriting. The first two cuttings reported the presence of Mr. and Mrs. Michael Burke in Venice and in Davos, in September 1938 and January 1939, respectively. The third was dated March 29, 1959. It read: "Many of our readers will mourn with us the passing of a bright star from the firmament of the European social scene. Mrs. Stella Burke, perhaps better known as Stella Harold Spenser, née Bellfort, died last Saturday in the nursing home near Lausanne,

Switzerland, where, sad to relate, she has spent the last three years. She was only sixty-six."

Beneath this Dr. Macfadden had ruled—with who knew what mixed emotions—his habitual line. Under it, the note read: "See Harold Spenser, Catherine."

Robert Hillier opened Catherine's file and turned to the back page. There he read, "Though I have obviously relied many times in these case histories on my own personal deductions, I have never resorted to guesswork nor quoted the deductions of others, however apt they may have seemed. This note is the sole exception; I enter it here because, if it is true, it explains much that has never been explained—at least to my satisfaction—about the Harold Spensers.

"My informant is normally accurate, and not of a gossiping frame of mind. That the information stems originally from a servant, and one who was dismissed by Michael Burke, may be thought to militate against it; but my informant assures me that there was no malice in the manner of its telling. (I should add that it is a story which I have heard from other, less reliable sources, and I must stress again that it is unconfirmed.)

"It is said that when Stella and Michael Burke returned from Mexico early in 1938, he was already conducting a love affair with his own stepdaughter, Catherine Harold Spenser, then seventeen.

"My notes on the character of the girl and of the man—my final meeting with Stella—her attitude to her daughter, which I noted at the time—the events which followed so swiftly after the arrival of Godfrey Bellfort that April: all these lend some credence to this monstrous story."

There was a double space; then: "Catherine Harold

Spenser died as a result of wounds received during the bombing of London in 1944. She was twenty-three years old."

Robert Hillier closed the files, arranged them in a neat pile and looked at them for a time; then he sighed and reached for a note pad; after a good deal of thought and several false starts he drafted the following telegram:

I AM MACFADDEN'S SON-IN-LAW AND INHERITED HIS PRACTICE STOP I HAVE SERIOUS PROBLEM REGARDING OWEN SPENSER FAMILY AND REGRET THAT YOUR PRESENCE HERE IS URGENTLY NECESSARY.

He addressed it to Godfrey Bellfort, care of his downtown office. (The private telephone numbers were still never divulged.)

For a moment he toyed with the idea of locking the Harold Spenser case histories in his office safe; then came to the conclusion that this would be risky; the idea that anyone might rob the place in search of money and so get hold of them made a cold sweat break out in the small of his back. As he packed them into his briefcase he could have sworn that they were actually hot to the touch.

Two

AT ABOUT the same time that Dr. Hillier was leaving his consulting room, the head librarian of the Lilienthal was soothing his bruised nerves with a strong bourbon, at the same time pacing about his luxurious office and muttering periodic imprecations directed at Richard Owen Spenser, who, during the interview which had just finished, had been at his most insufferable.

At the time that the documents in question had been withdrawn from the Spenser Collection it had never entered the head librarian's reasonable mind that anyone, but *anyone*, would ever presume to question Godfrey Bellfort, let alone use four-letter words about him. Times had changed since then, yes indeed; times, since then, had spawned and thrust upon the world a whole generation of Richard Owen Spensers, who did not, in his own words, "give a ten-cent fuck" for the values upon which the head librarian had based his life.

When he felt his nerves, and his hand, to be under sufficient control, he sat down at his desk, pulled a note pad towards him, and after a good deal of thought and several false starts, drafted the following telegram to Godfrey Bellfort, care of his downtown offices:

HAVE SERIOUS PROBLEM REGARDING OWEN SPENSER
FAMILY AND DOCUMENTS REMOVED FROM HERE AT

YOUR REQUEST STOP MY LEGAL POSITION UNTENABLE
STOP PLEASE INSTRUCT.

In every respect this chill grey January day was a
living fulfillment of the old adage about sleeping dogs
being allowed to lie. The Harold Spensers, all long
dead, were at it again. The uneasiness felt by Dr. Hillier
and the anger which had driven the head librarian of
the Lilienthal to the bourbon bottle were nothing
compared to the rage and frustration which gripped
Mrs. Amelia Guardi when she discovered, at six in the
evening, that Ellie, who had gone out with John Lamb
around midday, had not returned. She stilled the
panic-stricken thought that they might have disappeared for several days, even forever, but could not still
the restlessness which drove her from room to room,
from chair to chair. Ellie was necessary to the continu-
ation of her experiments, she no longer doubted that,
and she had no intention of repeating the unprofitable
experience of the previous night, with Lulu operating
on one cylinder (as it were) or not at all. She knew that
unless Ellie returned very soon, they would have to
abandon the evening's séance—tonight of all nights,
when it promised so much!—but she tried not to let her
overheated mind dwell on the fact.

Lulu, for her part, was just as frustrated by Ellie's
daylong absence—or rather, she was part frustrated
and part relieved, a dual emotion which was altogether
too much for her.

She had intended, as soon as Mrs. Guardi had
departed for the library, where she spent so much of
her time, to go across to the studio and warn the girl of
the danger which surrounded her; she knew this to be

her duty, not only to Ellie but to the powers which ruled her life. But it was patently impossible to warn Ellie when Ellie wasn't there, and Lulu knew enough about her own mental processes to be afraid that her resolve in this matter might weaken by tomorrow; she might even have mislaid the whole idea in that ragbag of jumbled thoughts which was her conscious mind.

On the credit side, however, she had come to realize —long after Amelia Guardi, needless to say—that the girl's continued absence would probably save her from the evening ritual of Fabergé Easter egg, candle, and trance; this would not only give her a rest, which she knew she needed, but time in which to consider what she really felt about the whole business. Many conflicting emotions were involved; the whole subject required careful thought and analysis: careful thought and analysis, as far as Lulu Jenkins was concerned, took a very very long time. She hoped that Ellie would stay away all night—for days perhaps.

Ellie and John Lamb walked in silence on a vast curve of grey deserted beach. A vicious north wind slashed at their faces and tried to tear their clothes from their backs. The Pacific, grey-black and in one of its murderous moods, thumped and thundered onto the sand, flinging fierce stinging whips of blown spray high overhead. The gulls screamed and wheeled in the teeth of the wind while small platoons of sandpipers performed their endless attack and hasty retreat at the foaming edge of each wave.

The young man and the girl paused and kissed; it was a long, loving kiss, and it seemed to infuriate the elements, bringing forth from the low sweeping clouds a sudden petulant scatter of rain.

Close to his ear, Ellie said, "John, we haven't made love for so long."

"I know it."

"Can we?"

Remembering the last time, remembering Hillier's warnings, he was troubled; but he managed to laugh. "What—*here*?"

Ellie laughed too, thinking of the welded lump of humanity rolling about on this wind-scraped beach, spray-spattered. But the urgency in both of them was real and painful. Lamb said, "You know what Hillier said."

"Hillier's old, he doesn't know what it's like." All the unknowing impatience of youth was in this. They clung together, feeling the weight of each thunderous wave as it struck the shuddering beach. The gulls dipped, screaming, over their heads.

John Lamb held out as long as he could; he kept her at Stinson Beach for dinner, but in a way this made it worse: it reminded them both too vividly of other lovers' dinners, fingers touching across the table, good wine sharpening the desire. They drove back slowly— even paused on the almost deserted bridge to feel it sway in the force of the gale; but eventually the car had to turn into the stable yard (watched from the big house by angry eyes); eventually he had to unlock the door and follow her into the warm and friendly room, where, through an open door, the warm and friendly bed beckoned to them.

Forgetting fear, forgetting doctors and cautions and

promises, they fell onto the bed and made love—beautiful, passionate, and uninhibited love.

Manlike, John Lamb was filled with a staggering sense of guilt in the instant after climax. But he need not have been afraid: the Ellie who lay in his arms was the Ellie he had always known and loved . . .

. . . and over in the big house, Lulu slept peacefully on her back, snoring rhythmically. The candle sat primly in its place on the bookcase, unlighted; the Fabergé egg lay in its velvet bag in a locked drawer in Mrs. Guardi's bedroom, while Mrs. Guardi herself . . .

Mrs. Guardi herself raved, restless and sleepless, about the silent house—from room to room, from chair to chair, from window to window. If only *she* possessed that vital power. If only! She opened the door of the big circular bedroom and looked into its haunted shadows; it was all there, she knew it; they were all there. Softly she called, "Michael? Michael Burke? I know you're there, I *know it!*"

She imagined she heard mocking laughter; if she did, it came from the street outside where somebody had come back, late, from a party.

The gale blew furiously all night, and by morning had exhausted itself. The sky was a hard, scoured blue; solid blocks of cloud sailed majestically across it, driven by an icy wind.

Mrs. Guardi, after some searching, found Lulu sitting on a hard chair in a corner of the big bedroom, staring into space. The fat body was slumped low, the chippolata-fingers were clasped upon her lap; the green eyes were closed, and from time to time the lips moved a little as if in silent prayer.

Amelia Guardi watched her for a while and then said very softly, "Lulu?" There was no response. She had to repeat the name three times in a crescendo before Mrs. Jenkins gave a slight start and turned the eyes upon her.

"I'm going to the library to do a little research."

There was no comprehension in the big woman's face—there seldom was on this subject.

"I want to see what I can find out about that girl, Lynne or Lynette, who was so . . . friendly with Michael Burke."

Lulu said, "Is there someone behind that door?"

It was impossible on these occasions not to feel a small *frisson* run up the spine; Mrs. Guardi felt it and was irritated by the sensation. "No, dear, of course not."

"She's always listening—always poking and prying."

"Who?"

"Catherine. Always listening behind doors. She moves so quietly. In a white dress."

Somewhere in the big circular room, Lulu (but not Mrs. Guardi) heard the distant echo of a voice: "Catherine, is that you? I know you're there—what are you doing? Catherine, go away!"

Long after the heavy front door had closed behind her employer, Lulu became properly aware of the fact that she was alone in the house. For a time she continued to sit in the corner while Stella Harold Spenser paced restlessly about the room, fighting those tears which she was always on the brink of shedding; meanwhile some other thought on some other plane kept nudging the edges of Lulu's subconscious. (Or maybe in her case the correct word was "consciousness," since what nagged her had to do with the present.) After a while it disentangled itself from the past, where Stella had once more flung herself onto the bed, sobbing helplessly; it was something that Lulu had to do—actually to *do*. Since she very seldom did anything very much, in the everyday sense of the word, whatever it was must be of enormous importance. Eventually it presented itself to her in all its clarity— and with all its unpleasant implications.

Lulu knew that she had to stand up and go to the door; go down the stairs and across the hall and out of the house—out of the house!—and then down to the stable yard, and then up those wooden stairs leading to the stable-studio. She had to speak to the girl; she had to warn her.

But supposing the young man was there? Or the brother? Or both? Lulu knew that she could probably just manage Ellie alone, but the idea of an audience, a crowd of young men, appalled her.

She continued to sit in the restless, murmuring room, trying to make up her mind—trying to rouse herself to take this action, which she knew to be very important —though she could not possibly guess how far-reaching its effect would be.

It was a good twenty minutes before the urgency of her thoughts communicated itself properly to her body. She sighed deeply and rose to her feet. There was somebody standing between herself and the door; she didn't like the feel of it at all, so it was probably the young man, Michael, come back to his wife with excuses, or presents, or, if he was drunk, vituperation.

She gave him a wide berth, went out of the door and closed it behind her, leaving the past to its own devious devices.

The cold wind smelled strongly of the sea. Lulu didn't notice heat or cold very much, but the smell stirred some old emotion in her which she could not define. (The suite which Jolly Jackie Jenkins had taken at the Martinez in Cannes had often smelled like that. Lulu was aware of faint personal pain, but unaware of the reason for it.)

In spite of her fears, Ellie was alone. She was cleaning out the studio, feeling better than she'd felt for days. Lulu Jenkins on her doorstep took her completely by surprise; and though she had seen her on three occasions, recognition came very slowly. They stared at each other, both uncertain.

"I need," said Lulu, "to speak to you." She glanced over her shoulder, and it struck Ellie suddenly that Mrs. Guardi was not intended to know about this visit.

"Come in, please. I'm sorry the place is such a mess." She stood out of the way.

Lulu took a single step forward and stopped abruptly. "Oh!"

"What's the matter?" She knew that the mess was not that bad. Lulu was peering into the room as if expecting it to explode in her face. Ellie had no means of knowing that this, in a way, was exactly what Mrs. Jenkins *was* expecting. After a moment she pulled herself together and entered the living room with enormous distaste considering how bright and pretty it looked in the sunshine, in spite of general untidiness.

Ellie was about to offer coffee when the big woman turned on her with extraordinary swiftness in one so

large and ungainly, and said, "I hadn't realized . . .
You must leave this place at once. Believe me, you
must go away from here—don't delay."

Ellie was speechless. Lulu Jenkins tore her strange
green eyes away from the disconcerted young face and
looked back at the room which offended her so much.
Then, again moving swiftly, she began to examine it in
detail, touching a wall here, a window there, pausing
for a long moment to stare at a point just to the right of
the bed. She then said something in French which Ellie
could barely catch. When she turned back, all color had
left the large and flaccid face; she looked deathly ill,
and almost instinctively Ellie pushed a chair towards
her. Lulu sat down, gasping. She was trying to remember what Mrs. Guardi had said the other night after
their séance. Ah yes, blood.

Ellie was alarmed. "Coffee," she said. "Would you
like some coffee?"

Lulu shook her head; she was in a hurry now; it was
essential that Mrs. Guardi did not find her here with
this girl. "The other night . . . you screamed, I think.
You were here at the door. You spoke of blood."

"Oh, that!" At the back of her mind Ellie was
thinking that her outburst must have frightened this
odd old creature. "I don't know what was the matter
with me."

"I do," said Lulu with unusual decision in her voice.
Ellie was again speechless. "For this reason it is
essential that you leave here."

"But I love it here, it's my home."

"There is danger—perhaps very great danger. You
must listen to me; many things here are beyond your
understanding."

"I don't know what you're talking about."

"I'm talking about you—about the way you have felt these past days. Don't tell me you have felt nothing!" There was no mistaking the sincerity, the knowledge that lay behind this.

Ellie said, "What do *you* know about the way I've been feeling? You . . ."

"Don't ask questions, I have no time; in any case, I cannot . . ." She shook the big head several times, so that tendrils of hair escaped the hairnet and fell about her face, giving her a quite demented look.

Ellie thought that perhaps this was the answer; and yet, how had she known . . . ? *What* exactly, for that matter, did she know? "All right, I have . . . I have been feeling pretty low for several days now. I don't see what it has to do with being here, or how you . . ."

"Please!" Lulu was on her feet again now; the pink ungainly hands wrestled with each other in anguish. "I cannot answer questions. Perhaps"—with a glance at the door—"perhaps I am wrong to be here. I beg you not to speak of it to anybody."

Ellie had recaptured her senses; she knew that "anybody" in this case meant Mrs. Amelia Guardi. Before she could frame another question, Lulu was on her way out. Ellie went after her. "Couldn't you . . . explain just a little? Why is it dangerous here?"

Lulu looked back at her from the door. "Go!" was all she said. "If you don't go . . ." Again she shook her head, lost for words or powerless to use them. "Believe me, I *know*."

More hair had escaped from the hairnet. The green eyes were fixed on Ellie in a terrible mute appeal; she realized that the eyes scared her—that the whole

persona of this sibylline apparition scared the hell out
of her; and at the same time she was sure that unlike
other people who used the expression "Believe me, I
know," Mrs. Jenkins was speaking the exact truth.
There was no doubt in Ellie's mind that she did
know—but what? It seemed that this question, like her
others, was going to remain forever unanswered, for
Lulu turned, opened the door, and, hair flying in the
chill wind, went thudding down the wooden stairs.

Ellie stood in the middle of her sunlit room, noticing
how the wind from the open door caught the vase of
narcissi on the bookcase, making them nod gracefully
as if they were growing in some quiet alpine pasture.
She knew that what had just happened was important,
even vitally important, but in some indefinable way she
didn't want to follow it up. Her visitor, that odd jumble
of a woman, had placed some kind of a key in her hand;
she had no idea what door it would open, but even if
the door in question faced her at this very moment, she
was pretty sure that she would not put the key in the
lock and open it; too many unknowable things—things
better left unknown perhaps—might lie on the other
side of it.

Suddenly, she was furiously angry. Tears of anger
gathered at the corner of her eyes. Wasn't that just like
life! Just when she felt so good! Just when she felt sane
and well for the first time in what seemed like eternity;
the loving of the night before, and of the morning, was
still powerfully with her, and here she was, cleaning
out her little home for the man she loved, knowing that
soon he would come back from his shopping, and take
her in his arms again—and they would be happy and
make love, and be happy and make love, without fear

. . . And now! Now fat Lulu had spoiled it all with her warnings and her mysteries.

Ellie felt inclined to keep the whole thing to herself; she felt that Lulu's visit, well-intentioned or not, had constituted an invasion of her innermost privacy. What she didn't realize was that this feeling in itself was part of the danger that Lulu Jenkins had been talking about.

The thunder had rolled on Olympus, the lightning had flashed, and Godfrey Bellfort, made human, now stood gazing out of the library window of the vast mansion which was his San Franciscan home, if "home" was the right name for a house which he had visited three times in the past ten years. This was a cold god, compared with those all-too-fallible Greeks who had cavorted on Mount Olympus. Watching the divine back, Robert Hillier wondered whether this man had ever loved anybody, whether anybody had ever loved him; it seemed impossible.

There were several other Bellfort "homes" dotted about the globe. Very few people knew exactly where they were; a chosen few must have actually visited them—so carefully chosen and so few that no word of the experience ever escaped to the outside world. The media had long ago given up the effort; deprived of its idiot chatter, the media-fed masses didn't even know that Godfrey Bellfort existed, which was exactly what he had in mind. He viewed the antics of other rich men with distaste; the histrionic isolation of a Hughes was, in his opinion, beneath contempt, and he felt that the Gettys could perfectly well keep their name out of the newspapers if it suited them to do so. On the whole he found the behavior of the rich infinitely more common than the behavior of the so-called "common man." Did he collect paintings, wives, diamonds, mistresses, icons, boys, butterflies? Nobody knew.

He turned and looked at Dr. Hillier; it was, Hillier thought, an unknowable face—slightly, but not vulgarly, tanned, eyes of a pale hard grey, designed for outstaring basilisks, a firm straight mouth with neither an upward lift of humor about it nor a downward slant of melancholy; the steel-white hair was neatly cut; the suit was grey, the tie was black, the shirt was white. In the elegant umber-ish luxury of this library he looked as singular and sharply out of place as a jagged piece of granite in a whore's bed.

He came back into the room, moving with what could only be called economy, though his slim exercised body gave no indication of his age (which Hillier had estimated to be seventy-two). His voice was cool, unhurried, devoid of revelations: "You say both these young men are determined."

"Very."

"That's encouraging. I didn't know there were any determined young men left. Angry, rebellious . . ." There was a faint sardonic overtone to these two words. "But determined . . . ! Well, well!"

Would he, Hillier wondered, be quite so cool, quite so patronizing when faced with Richard Owen Spenser? It remained to be seen.

Bellfort had picked up a piece of paper from the desk; he handed it to the other man. Hillier read, "Have serious problem regarding Owen Spenser family and documents removed from here at your request. My legal position untenable. Please instruct." He recognized the name at the end of it. "The Lilienthal."

"Correct. No doubt I would have been wise to have destroyed those documents with your father-in-law's case histories when I had the opportunity."

Hillier said nothing. He was wondering when, or if, this cold hard man was going to say anything about the matter which lay at the crux of the whole situation—that there was, that there had to be, a taint of insanity in the Bellfort family.

"I shall need to meet these two . . . determined young men, of course. Not here."

"At my house."

"That would be admirable. There are certain inquiries I wish to make first. Let us say three o'clock this afternoon."

He was not to know whether at three o'clock that afternoon Robert Hillier was inextricably pledged to . . . what? His daughter's birthday party, a desperately ailing patient, a summons to the White House, a death, for God's sake. No matter, Bellfort had spoken.

As he left the vast house he remembered what old Dr. Macfadden had written all those years ago: "Age has only polished the steel of that character . . . though one could never like him, it is impossible to *dis*like him—he is so complete."

As well as a large quantity of food, John Lamb had brought Ellie's brother back with him from his shopping expedition. In spite of that reluctance, which she still felt, Ellie had immediately told them about Lulu's extraordinary visit. The countless permutations introduced into the puzzle by this new factor were still racing through their brains.

"She said there was danger, and I must leave here at

once—and she wouldn't answer any questions. She seemed . . . scared."

"Scared?"

"I don't think Mrs. Guardi knew she was here; she kept looking towards three-three-seven."

Lamb went to the window and stared up at the blank façade of the big house, at the heavily ornamented cornice and the two towers which had once struck him as so absurdly endearing. "I wonder what the hell those two old birds are up to?"

"Get hold of Lulu and grill her?" suggested Richie.

"No." Ellie shook her head. "She isn't talking, I can tell you that for sure; she'll clam up." Richie looked at her with raised brows. Ellie elaborated. "She may be old and she may be as batty as hell, but she . . . There's something strong about her. Something a bit frightening, I guess."

Richie looked at Lamb. "Put on our Sherlock hats and get in there with our magnifying glasses?"

Lamb turned and their eyes met. "Can we?" He nodded towards the house. "The downstairs windows are all barred, and I don't know about you, but I'm no cat burglar."

Ellie said, "There's an alarm on every window that'd wake the dead—forget it."

Lamb came and sat down on the sofa next to her; he put an arm around her shoulder and she leaned her head against him; but he could feel the tension in her; the muscles of her back were hard; he knew, with a sinking of the heart, that the freedom and spontaneity of last night had disappeared again. Into his shoulder she said, "You could *walk* in if the key to that closet in the bedroom wasn't lost."

"Jesus! Why didn't I think of that?" Richie disappeared into the bedroom. Lamb kissed Ellie gently on the lips, and was glad to feel, in spite of the tension, a quick eager response.

The closet in question was not really a closet at all; at some time it had been a way into the studio which did not necessitate going round via the front of the big house and the stable yard; it consisted of two doors enclosing a tiny lobby. On the studio side the door was open; on the house side it was locked; the space between was full of Ellie's clothes. John Lamb stood looking at them while Richie inspected the locked door—clothes that held warm memories for him, clothes that she had worn in Paris in happier times; he let his cheek rest against the yellow coat, remembering a laughing day at Longchamps.

Richie straightened up from the heavy old mortice lock. "Well, at least it's on this side—we can unscrew it if we have to." With his usual acuity he had seen and recognized the expression on the other man's face. More gently he said, "She's going to be okay. We're going to lick this thing, I know it."

Lamb nodded. Richie grinned. "I have to tell you this is the first time I've ever been shut up in a closet with a handsome guy and not tried to make him."

From the living room, Ellie called out, "I've just had an idea."

Richie shouted back, "So have I," still grinning.

"I mean, about how you can get into the house. It's easy."

Amelia Guardi did not always come back to 337 Gilman Street for lunch, but on this particular day she made a point of doing so. There were several reasons for this. In the first place, Ellie's disappearance the day before had unsettled her profoundly, more than she had realized at the time. Long after the girl had returned, long after she had finished prowling restlessly about the big house, she had found herself unable to sleep: too many uncomfortable thoughts were running about like mice in the upper attics of her mind.

As a result, she had not gone to the library that morning to continue her famous "research," but had sat for two and a half hours in the lounge of the St. Francis Hotel drinking strong black coffee. During this time she had pursued and rounded up all the mice. Three facts emerged. In the first place, Ellie Owen Spenser was vitally necessary to their exploration of the past. Secondly, Lulu had developed a moral reluctance to making use of this God-given opportunity even though she readily admitted that the girl acted as a kind of booster to her psychic powers. Thirdly, and in conclusion, Mrs. Guardi had no intention of putting up with such nonsense. Ellie must be used and used to the full. (She did not spend one of these endless minutes of thought in considering the danger to which Ellie would be exposed by such "use.")

Mrs. Guardi was a woman who made careful plans and carried them out to the letter and to their conclusion. That there was something almost manic in her determination did not worry her; in this flabby and directionless world, it was the only way to get things done; it was true that occasionally other people had to suffer, but then people had always had to suffer for any great cause. History was full of examples.

Lunch was a silent meal—it usually was, but on this occasion the silence was charged with overtones. Lulu had not altogether recovered from her foray into the outside world, and though she had long ago felt various things emanating from the direction of the studio, the actual impact of the place had astonished her by its violence; it had even given her a nasty headache. She hadn't yet realized that all this was merely an extension of the moral problem and would have to be dealt with accordingly, but the thought was fighting its way to the surface of her mind.

Amelia Guardi watched the precious lump covertly; she looked unusually ill today; if only she would occasionally go out and get some air—or eat less! The much-desired end was already in sight, she was sure of that; she had glimpsed the oasis between two burning mountains of sand—the camel must *not* be allowed to let her down at the last moment. Mrs. Guardi had no intention of dying for lack of water when water lay just over the next hill. Equally she knew that the next, the last, hill was a steep one fraught with danger; she must proceed very carefully indeed.

She made no reference to this problem, but allowed herself to say, towards the end of the meal, "Now Lulu, make sure that you have a really good rest this afternoon; I have a feeling that tonight will be decisive, one might almost say the turning point, don't you agree?"

Lulu grunted through a mouthful of ice cream; the pale-green eyes were evasive. "Where will you be?"

"Back at my research," said Mrs. Guardi firmly. "The time is very near now, Lulu my dear, when we must sit down to the task of actually writing our book; we must be absolutely sure of all our facts."

Mrs. Jenkins nodded glumly. Book, facts . . . that appalling room . . . a turning point, don't you agree? . . . the girl's face, staring in surprise and perhaps fear . . . research, facts, our book . . . our book . . . our book . . . Lulu grappled with her tumbling thoughts, wondering which of them it was that nagged at her like an aching tooth.

As for Mrs. Guardi, she could not say that she felt any more secure than before lunch, but at least the camel had not balked at the *idea* of the steep and dangerous hill. It would have to be led carefully, perhaps bullied a little; she knew that she would probably, as so often in the past, be seized by the desire to beat it black and blue, but then, camels, as the world knew, were not easily intimidated; they were contrary mammals, quite capable of reacting to a beating by settling their ungainly rumps upon the sand and refusing to budge so much as an inch.

As she nodded to the chauffeur and climbed into the back of the rented limousine which would whisk her down to the library, Mrs. Guardi was saying to herself, "But whatever happens, there *will* be a séance tonight, she *will* do as I say!" She did not notice (how could she possibly have suspected?) that John Lamb and Richard Owen Spenser were sitting in the latter's car, parked by the roadside a hundred yards behind the limousine. When that majestic vehicle moved slowly away, turned a corner, and disappeared from sight, both young men got out of the car quickly and approached Number 337.

Richie stood to one side while Lamb mounted the steps and rang the doorbell.

If Lulu had already arranged herself supine upon her comfortable bed, she would probably have ignored the shrill summons of the bell, but it caught her with one foot on the bottom stair. She was not in the habit of opening the door; nothing that went on outside it was of any particular interest to her; she looked at it blankly. The bell rang again.

Lulu felt a compulsion to open it—something to do with her morning's sortie perhaps; she thumped across the hall and did so. Lamb casually inserted a foot into the gap thus created, and said with as much boyish charm as he could muster, "You remember me, Miss Owen Spenser's friend—I borrowed some books from you the other day and wanted to return them." He raised a little the four volumes under his arm.

Lulu wavered uncertainly. In her deepest mind this young man was inextricably confused with that other, that Michael, Mikey, that dark shadow; she peered at this one suspiciously, not looking at him so much as assessing him; she was surprised to find only lightness, something firm and perhaps even pleasing—certainly no evil. She opened the door wider and said, "Yes," waving a fat and ill-formed hand towards the inside of the house.

"Thank you so much."

Lulu watched him go quickly across the hall and up the stairs. The confusion, she decided, must be entirely within herself, and yet she had seemed to detect it in the young girl as well. She shrugged, sighing deeply. The problem might solve itself later, if she remembered it; at the moment the other was more pressing. What other? How she wished she were lying on her bed! She was exhausted—perhaps even unwell. She had felt like

this before, but when? She had forgotten when, which
was probably just as well; it had been when Jackie
Jenkins had pushed her to the limits of endurance, thus
destroying the power that was in her and killing the
golden goose into the bargain.

She was about to close the door, prior to following
John Lamb upstairs, when Richard Owen Spenser, just
behind her, said, "Good afternoon, Mrs. Jenkins—I
thought I'd come over to see about that damp."

Damp! Lulu turned ponderously, by which time
Richie was already inside the house. "In the big salon, I
believe."

Big salon? Damp? Which one was this? Oh yes, the
brother. He was already moving towards the room on
the opposite side of the hall to the dining room, the
room they never used. At the door, he turned to her,
smiling. "Perhaps you'd care to show me?" He beckoned, and Lulu drifted towards him, as she tended to
drift towards any quick and decisive force. As for
damp, she had no idea what he was talking about . . .

Upstairs, Lamb could hear all this going on. He did
not know what he expected to find; they had none of
them been able to decide what it might be that he was
to look for—anything unusual, had been the final
decision, a vague one.

If Lulu succeeded in breaking away from Richie and
came upstairs, Lamb must be found in the room which
Mrs. Guardi had told him she called "the study."
Knowing Richie, he doubted that Lulu would do any
breaking away until that young man was good and
ready—which meant, on Lamb's own reappearance
downstairs. However, he decided to inspect the bedrooms first; the ones in use were instantly recogniz-

able; they made an interesting contrast. Amelia Guardi must, on a conservative estimate, have had five times more clothing and personal possessions than Lulu Jenkins, but Mrs. Guardi's room was a model of tidiness whereas Mrs. Jenkins' room was, as Lamb the Londoner put it to himself, "a right old mess." Neither room revealed anything that the two women themselves did not make plain at first sight: Mrs. Guardi was fastidious and rich, Lulu was a muddler and poor. One of Mrs. Guardi's immaculately tidy drawers was locked, but then, Mrs. Guardi was the kind of lady who would carry traveler's checks, bank statements, credit cards, and possibly a considerable sum in cash. Lamb was sure that a professional detective might learn a great deal from all this; he himself learned nothing.

As he crossed the hall towards the study he heard Richie saying, "I was *sure* the agent said 'damp.' I own other property, you know, I wonder if he was referring to that."

The first thing that Lamb noticed about the study was that the Fabergé Easter egg no longer stood on the little table by the window; he was sorry about this, as he had promised himself a closer look at it. He returned the books to their shelf and began to inspect the room more carefully. There was a single candlestick at one end of the bookcase; the candle had burned down to within an inch or two of its base; this struck him as odd. Anybody might burn candles in the dining room, but why up here? Unless, of course, the lights had fused.

He continued his search. It seemed to him that there was nothing else in the least unusual about the comfortable and much-used room: a biography open and face downwards on the arm of one of the easy chairs (Mrs. Guardi), a jumble of inexpert crochet on a table beside the other (who else but Lulu?), a pack of cards spread on the green baize of . . . But why a tape recorder? He examined it more closely: a good tape recorder but a small one—too small (as he, a music buff, well knew) for the adequate reproduction of music, particularly the kind of music that Mrs. Amelia Guardi would assuredly like, i.e., classical. A tape recorder for speech then. Whose speech?

The answer lay on a lower shelf of the bookcase: a neat row of tapes in their boxes. Squatting, he saw that there were ten of them in all. Six of the ten boxes were marked with a number; nothing else, simply a number; the other four were blank.

John Lamb considered them for a moment; then he took box number four from the shelf, opened it, removed the tape and put it in his pocket; next he subtracted the unused tape from the box at the end of the row, placed it in box number four, returned both boxes to their respective positions and straightened up, pleased with himself. On second thoughts he decided that if he himself reached for an unused tape, he would probably take the one on the end, so he moved the empty box to position number eight. If of course anybody wanted to play back tape number four, they would immediately find that it had mysteriously become blank; further investigation would then reveal the empty box, and suspicion would obviously fall on himself, the interloper. That was a risk he had to take, and a contingency he would deal with if it ever arose.

He selected three more books from the shelf by the door—in order to justify the length of time he had been upstairs—and went back to the hall, where Richie was now explaining to a bemused and perhaps frantic Mrs. Jenkins the problems of damp-courses in old houses. They greeted each other with appropriate surprise, Lamb showed his books to Lulu, and they left the house together. Lulu closed the door firmly after them, determined never to answer the bell again. All this contact with the outside world, so noisy and so relentlessly practical, had made her feel like a warrior returned from battle; she dragged herself up to her bed, fell onto it, pulling the quilt up to her chin, and was asleep within five minutes, mercifully unaware of the recorded performance she was about to give in Richie's apartment not too far away.

If Ellie had possessed a tape recorder, they would have taken their loot directly to the studio. (Later they were going to be thoroughly relieved that they had not done so; even more relieved that Ellie had made an appointment to have her hair done, and was therefore not available to accompany them.)

However, they had hardly set out for Russian Hill before Lamb said, "Oh hell!"

Richie glanced at him; he was staring gloomily at the reel of tape. "Mrs. Guardi's a writer—she told me so the first time I went over there."

"So?"

"All we've got is probably a bunch of notes for some dreary book."

"If she's a writer, what's Lulu?"

Lamb couldn't answer this one. Richie continued: "Also, if she's a writer, I'll eat my hat—my fur one."

Since tape number four began with Lulu's extraordinary and realistic representation of a young girl engaged in the act of copulation, it immediately became obvious that Richie's fur hat was perfectly safe. He and John Lamb sat on opposite sides of the room (no sign of Stefan, who had presumably been given his marching orders, as planned) and listened in blank astonishment, eyes wide.

"Jesus!" said Richie. "They're a couple of old pornos!"

"But don't you see what's so odd?"

They listened to the rhythmic gasping and panting, the murmured endearments choked by moans of pleasure. Richie nodded. "You mean it's only her. No man."

"No man and no bed."

The lady on the tape recorder reached her rather noisy climax and subsided slowly. There was a pause, a long pause broken only by the gentle whisper of blank tape. Then, suddenly, a woman's voice, taut with fear, said, "Who's that?"

Both young men started involuntarily. After another moment's silence: "Go away! Get away from that door!" The sound of rapid breathing. "I know you're there—go away, go away!" The breathing continued for a while; then faded slowly to silence. Out of which yet another voice, unmistakably that of a child, began to chant, "Piggy's fallen downstair-airs, Piggy's fallen downstair-airs . . ."

Lamb ran a hand through his hair in a mute gesture of frustration. "What in God's name . . . ?"

"Ssh!"

The child's voice sighed deeply and added in a mournful tone, *"Poor* Piggy!"

Richie turned to Lamb, blue eyes very brilliant. "Piggy—don't you remember Piggy?"

Lamb looked blank.

"That day at the Lilienthal. Piggy was Patrick's nickname. Patrick—Stella's child who died!"

"Blimey!"

The London exclamation was drowned by a terrifying cry of rage from the tape recorder: "Bitch, bitch, bitch—I know you're there! Come here, come here at once! Catherine, do you hear me—come here at once!"

"Catherine." It was Lamb who exclaimed this time; their eyes met.

The woman's voice began to moan—a terrible lost moan of mortal pain, unbearable pain: "You're lying, you always lie. I won't listen. No, don't tell me these things, I won't listen—you're lying and I won't listen." The voice choked back a sob. "I don't care, I don't want to know, I won't listen. Stop, Catherine, stop—I won't listen, it's all lies . . . lies . . . lies . . ." The voice was choked by sobs. The sobbing went on a long time.

Richie said, "I don't . . . I don't think I believe in this kind of thing."

"Spiritualism?"

Richie nodded. The sobbing continued. "It has to be something like that."

Lamb considered for a moment. "Somehow it . . . it does fit those two women."

"You're darn right it does. Who'd have a female like Lulu as a companion? She's practically a half-wit."

"Mrs. Guardi wouldn't."

"That's for sure."

They both listened to the sobs coming from the tape

recorder. They rose and fell; died away into sniffling, and broke out into fresh paroxysms of misery. Once the woman's voice cried, quietly and venemously, "Bitch! Bitch!" before relapsing into another welter of tears.

Lamb said, "So you think Lulu's a . . . what do they call it?"

"Medium—yes I do."

Lamb said again, "It fits." He was surprised to find how easily the fantastic could be assimilated; perhaps mankind was aware of more things than he allowed himself to admit. "You mean, this is her now?"

The sobbing reached another crescendo. Richie said, "Well . . . not exactly *her*."

Suppressing a small shudder, because he himself knew what he thought to be the answer, Lamb said, "Who then?"

After a long moment's thought, Richie sighed. "Stella Harold Spenser, who else?"

The sobbing stopped abruptly. There was a dead, waiting silence. The two young men looked towards the gently turning spools of the tape recorder. It rewarded them with a shriek that made Richie say, "Christ!" and Lamb jerk forward in his chair. Then, in what was obviously abject terror, the same woman's voice screamed, "For God's sake, there's blood all over your hands. No—don't touch that *knife!*"

Lamb was on his feet. Richie went quickly to the machine and pressed the *Pause* button. He straightened up and they faced each other; there was no need for either of them to mention the two incidents with which Ellie had shocked them so deeply—the incident of the knife, and the incident of the bloodstained room.

Richie said, "It's them—it's nothing to do with insanity; it started soon after they took the house, she was perfectly okay till then."

The inferences, the ramifications were too much for Lamb; he burst out, "But that's impossible . . . !"

"So ESP's impossible, ghosts are impossible, poltergeists are impossible! You don't believe in them and I don't believe in them, but thousands of people do."

John Lamb shook his head, possibly in disbelief, possibly to clear it of a mess of preconceived notions.

"Maybe," said Richie grimly, "we're about to join the ranks of the believers."

"What are we going to do?"

"Break into that darned house when they're at it, and see just what goes on."

"Are you sure we can get the lock off?"

The telephone cut short Richie's answer. Proof of their utter involvement, if proof were needed, lay in the fact that both young men looked instinctively, not at the telephone but at the tape recorder.

It was Dr. Hillier. He'd called both Richie's apartment and the studio perhaps half an hour before—there had been no answer from either. He was glad to have reached Richie because he wanted to see them quite urgently; could they possibly get over there right away, at least by three o'clock?

Richie said that they'd be delighted to go over right away; he added that they themselves had discovered something that might conceivably interest Hillier.

Robert Hillier would have suggested his Sutter Street consulting room and not his house for this meeting if there had been any chance of Betty Hillier being at home; but she had announced that morning that she was going over to Burlingame to visit her sister; they had not seen each other for three weeks; her husband knew that there must be a backlog of gossip which would keep her there until an hour or so before dinner.

He did not warn Richie and Lamb, on opening the front door, of what awaited them in the drawing room. The expression on Richie's face when he introduced them to Godfrey Bellfort repaid, in Hillier's opinion, some of the things that young man had said to him the other day.

Bellfort, who had remained seated, emperor-like, regarded his raw material with granite eyes which betrayed nothing. Richard Owen Spenser said, "Bellfort! Well, well—that hunk of lard down at the Lilienthal really got moving, didn't he?"

"I think he found you reasonably alarming," Bellfort replied evenly. "He has never been a man of much character." In this way he managed to warn Richie that other men, himself for example, were less impressionable. "I gather you want to see the documents which I asked to be removed."

"Not much. But I want to know what right *you* think you have to remove them."

Hillier, safe in his ringside seat, could not help admiring the young man; could not, in a way, help being touched by his youth, which he flung so gallantly and so foolishly at the old tungsten-faced, unbelievably powerful man who faced him. He even winced a little in anticipation of the coming blow which would, he felt sure, knock Master Owen Spenser over the ropes and out for the count.

In a tone of the utmost mildness Godfrey Bellfort

replied, "I had no right. I did so to protect the memory of my sister, whom I loved very much—wouldn't you have done the same for yours?"

Silence. So this, Hillier was thinking—when his thought processes had recovered sufficiently—this is the secret at the heart of the Bellfort legend. The man is quite simply a genius.

Before Richie had found his voice, Bellfort added, "She was, as you must already know, a very sick woman, afflicted with a brain disorder which ultimately destroyed her."

Robert Hillier, the sailor, could remember many a day of fine sailing when suddenly the wind had not so much died as disappeared completely from the face of the sea, leaving the sails inert, the yacht wallowing, much as young Richard now wallowed inert in the center of this room.

John Lamb, partly out of sympathy for Richie, cleared his throat and said, "In any case, we've discovered that . . . that something else, something quite different, is probably responsible for Ellie's . . . state of mind."

"That would have to be the explanation; she is in no way related to my family." He stretched out a long lean hand towards the fire that burned in the big hearth. "Having said which . . ." Hillier noticed a touch of cold steel creeping back into the voice which had, a few seconds ago, been simply that of a sad old man. "Having said which, I must add that the admission I have just made in this room, regarding my sister's mental health, is the only such admission that has ever been made—possibly the only one that ever *will* be made."

Richie's head had jerked up. Bellfort gave him an icy look. "This, I'm sure, is much more the kind of thing you expected to hear from me; I'm glad not to disappoint you." He looked towards the side of the ring. "Hillier is a doctor—he is used to keeping secrets . . ."

And would, Hillier was thinking, lose his practice very swiftly if he didn't.

"Which means," Bellfort continued, eying the two young men with an indifferent eye, "that if any word of what I've said ever reached the . . . the outside world, it would be through the indiscretion of one or other of *you*. I would take immediate action, and you would, I assure you, regret it."

The grey merciless eyes looked from Lamb's brown ones to Richie's hard azure stare. A log settled in the grate and threw up a cheery fountain of sparks.

Hillier now discovered that if Godfrey Bellfort could astound him, so too could Richard Owen Spenser; for that young man suddenly threw back his head and let out a gusty laugh of pure enjoyment. Bellfort almost but not quite showed surprise. Gasping, Richie said, "Jesus, you're great—you're absolutely great!"

John Lamb was struck, as he had never been struck before, by the foreign-ness of these people; he found it in a way heartwarming. Language tended to make the British think of the Americans as kin; they were not—they were utterly different, and in many ways (he was forced to admit it) bigger.

For the Anglo-Saxons, however, he decided to intervene with a little reason. He said to the intimidating foreigner in the big chair by the fire, "You're wrong, I'm afraid, in thinking that we're the only people around with any evidence of your sister's state of mind.

I'd hate to become your enemy because of the . . . indiscretion of a pair of batty old women."

The grey eyes hardened. Richie's amusement died abruptly; he said, "Oh God, yes."

Bellfort leaned forward. "What exactly do you mean by that?"

Lamb told him.

It happened that Mrs. Guardi, who had just returned from her afternoon's "research," noticed the beautiful Rolls as it turned the corner and stole silently down Gilman Street. The fact that Amelia Guardi, who was not interested in motorcars and who owned a Rolls herself, paused to watch it indicates the kind of car it was. She was intrigued to observe that it was slowing down as it approached Number 337.

She moved into the study to confirm her impression that it was in fact sliding to a halt in front of the house; this is exactly what it now did. The car was in two shades of brown, deep chestnut and something nearly black; the chauffeur matched the chestnut. He opened a door and Godfrey Bellfort got out, crossed the sidewalk, and mounted the steps. Mrs. Guardi frowned to herself. A second later the doorbell rang.

Lulu was still, audibly, taking her siesta. Mrs. Guardi, though not used to that kind of thing, went downstairs, crossed the hall, taking a quick look at her appearance in the big mirror as she did so, and, satisfied with what she saw, opened the door.

Godfrey Bellfort looked up at her. It would probably be true to say that never in its seventy-two years had his face registered anything like the expression of pure shock which crossed it at the sight of the woman who confronted him, smiling very slightly.

"Catherine!" He put out an old man's hand to steady himself on the doorpost. "Catherine Harold Spenser."

"Yes," said Mrs. Guardi.

Part I V

THE
COMING
TOGETHER

One

THEY FACED each other in the chill, unlived-in spaces of the big downstairs room that had always been called "the salon." Mrs. Guardi would have preferred the warmth of the small study, but it was too close to Lulu, who would, if not disturbed by raised voices, sleep until aroused to partake of food. In a way the echoing limbo of the big room, which she had never liked even as a child, seemed as good a place as any for this meeting. Dusk was already falling outside, but that suited the meeting too; she made no effort to turn on any lights.

Godfrey Bellfort stood in his immaculately tailored, immaculately conservative overcoat, looking out of a window into the tangled, once-beautiful garden which they had both known so well, a long time ago. Mrs. Guardi, born Catherine Harold Spenser, waited patiently and without uneasiness until he had regained enough control of himself to turn towards her; even then he could not keep the edge of a trembling anger out of his voice: "This is monstrous. Why didn't you tell me . . . ?"

"Why should I tell you anything—what has it to do with you?"

"Everything—as you well know."

The woman smiled; it was the same quiet smile of

satisfaction with which she had greeted him. "Did you think I was dead?"

"Everybody thought you were dead."

"I happened to be in London at the time of the bombing. It seemed a good opportunity to get away from . . . oh, a lot of things, you in particular." Still smiling, she added, "How easy it is for a woman to disappear; she just changes her name by getting married, and goes to live in another place."

"You had children?"

"With your sister for a mother!" The venom was almost visible in the nearly dark room. "We adopted two boys; they're nice and sane."

Godfrey Bellfort took an angry pace towards her, and checked himself. His expression was hidden by growing darkness, but she could imagine it. A foghorn wailed dismally in the distance. Fog was probably at that moment stealing in through the Golden Gate, spreading over the Bay.

Bellfort said, "What are you doing here?"

"Minding my own business. Don't worry, I'm not interested in giving away any dirty family secrets."

"I was told that you're writing a book. What book?"

"Of course I'm not writing a book." The scorn was absolute. "I needed some kind of an excuse. Who have you been talking to?"

"That doesn't matter."

Mrs. Guardi thought for a moment; then shrugged. "No, I don't suppose it does."

"There's a woman here with you—does she know who you are?"

"She doesn't know who I *was*."

Bellfort came forward, peering at the well-preserved,

still-beautiful face in what remained of daylight. "What else does she know?" The woman did not reply. "You're messing about with some kind of spiritualist nonsense."

"It's not nonsense."

"Is she a medium?"

"Yes."

"Does she . . . know what happened?"

Mrs. Guardi smiled again. "That's a very interesting question; she does and she doesn't."

"You still can't give a direct answer, you haven't changed."

"Neither have you."

"Answer my question—does she know?"

"She knows everything . . . and she knows nothing. In her capacity as a medium she's quite extraordinary; as a human being she's a moron. She has no memory of what she does or says, and as for writing a book . . . !" Mrs. Guardi's voice seemed to relish the contempt she had been forced to hide for so long. "She couldn't write a postcard."

Bellfort said, "Catherine . . . ?"

"Don't call me Catherine, I always did hate it. My name is Amelia—Amelia Guardi."

"Catherine, I want you to go away from this house, away from San Francisco altogether."

"No."

"Can't you see the danger?"

"There's no danger."

"There is. People . . . Certain people are talking about you already. If they find out who you are, what you're doing here . . ." He left this in midair; presumably both of them could understand very clearly what this discovery would mean.

After a moment Mrs. Guardi said, "They won't."

"Somebody could recognize you in the street—anybody, an old friend, even a servant."

"I thought you'd . . . taken care of all the servants."

"Don't be obtuse—*anyone* could recognize you, follow you, find out that you're living in the same *house*, for God's sake!" No one who knew or had known Godfrey Bellfort in "the outside world" which he despised so much could ever have recognized the stricken voice that now came out of near-darkness— nor the tone which was remarkably close to pleading.

With maddening placidity Mrs. Guardi replied, "People don't recognize a dead woman."

"I did—at once."

"You have a good reason to."

The bitterness in this seemed to silence him for a moment. When he spoke again he sounded utterly weary—a weary old man of seventy-two. "Can't you even appreciate what would happen if the newspapers got to hear?"

Sudden rage surged out of the gloom at him: "Stella, Stella, Stella! Jesus Christ, you'd think she was still alive, the way you fuss about her! What does it matter, what does *she* matter any more? She's dead, Godfrey, dead and gone—there's nothing for you or any of the other idiots to love any more."

Again Bellfort was silent. This time the voice had regained some of its steel. "Is it money you want?"

Mrs. Guardi laughed. "I'm a rich woman, thank you very much." He felt rather than saw that she had walked past him to the window; he turned; she now stood in silhouette, looking out at the tangled garden where she had played as a child. "I'm staying here until I . . . achieve what I came here to achieve."

"Which is?"

He was answered by silence. Still looking out of the window, she eventually said, "Go away, Godfrey—there's nothing you can do here. You can't bully me and you can't blackmail me, not any more."

"I wouldn't be too sure of that." It was once again the voice that the outside world would recognize—steely, blank, and incisive; the cold empty room resounded with it.

The woman swung around and stared into the darkness; then, very swiftly, she came back towards him, moving between pieces of furniture as surely as a cat. "I said I wasn't *interested* in telling any family secrets; that doesn't mean I give a damn one way or the other. Don't worry me, Godfrey, and don't threaten me, or I just might hold open house and tell everybody in this whole stinking town everything I know—how would you like that?"

"You wouldn't dare. You're guilty, Catherine, and don't you forget it!"

"You're as guilty as I am, Godfrey Bellfort." She was very close to him now; he could smell her perfume, and could see, pinpointed in each dark eye, the pale reflection of the window. "Which guilt would they find more interesting—little old Amelia Guardi, the housewife from Boston, Mass.—or the great, unknown God Bellfort, is he or isn't he the richest man in the world?"

They faced each other in the darkness. The woman laughed again, softly.

● ● ●

John Lamb and Richard Owen Spenser knelt on the floor in Ellie's clothes closet. Ellie, clutching a swathe of dresses to her chest, watched them. They had only given her a very general impression of what the stolen tape had told them; she could guess, from their intent expressions as they worked on the door if from nothing else, that there was a good deal they were holding back. The malady which had gripped her and which seemed to grip her no more had, by its very nature, been less alarming for her than for them; in fact, she could hardly remember anything about it. Therefore, their work on the door—their whole plan of investigating more closely what went on in the big house— seemed to her to have that inessential quality which, for women, often attends a great many male activities.

Ellie had no particular feeling one way or the other about psychic phenomena; again like most women, she had a vague feeling that "there was probably something in it," and the idea that some sixth sense in her had become involved with whatever Lulu and Mrs. Guardi were up to made limited sense. As far as she was concerned, only two things really mattered: she was no longer ill, and her fear of inherited insanity seemed to have no foundation whatever; but then, Ellie herself had not seen her own body writhing on a bed in some terrifyingly prolonged sexual spasm; she had not witnessed her own lumpish and uncharacteristic withdrawal from her surroundings and everybody who inhabited them, nor the witless terror she had shown on seeing her apartment covered in blood which had not been there; she certainly didn't know that her words on that occasion had been the exact words spoken (if the tape could be believed) by Stella Harold

Spenser some thirty-odd years before.

The lock had proved a problem from the moment it had first been attacked; it was thickly coated with many layers of paint, and the screws had reacted typically, not only to the damp ocean air of San Francisco, but to the fact that they had been left alone for so many years in an unheated part of an abandoned house. At one point they had proved so recalcitrant that Lamb had been forced to go out onto the wooden staircase with a hammer, and effect mock repairs in order to mask the noise which Richie was making in Ellie's bedroom.

Luckily, the door on its other side was at the end of more than one unused corridor, and since this had once been the nursery part of the big house, in a far-off and happy day when children had been seen more than heard, there was a heavy door covered in red baize separating it from the rooms inhabited by Mrs. Guardi and Lulu. In fact, all these precautions were unnecessary, since Mrs. Guardi had been out and Lulu lost in an abyss of slumber from which nothing, let alone a mere hammer on iron, could ever have awakened her.

Now, at last, the lock was free of the door. Lamb unscrewed their side of the handle, and Richie manipulated the tongue out of its cavity; they could now walk at will into 337 Gilman Street, but must first hide the evidence of their handiwork. They left the lock hanging in position and replaced the door handle so that the one on the other side wouldn't give them away by its crookedness; they then bolted the door with the heavy bolt which Lamb had fixed during the afternoon. Now, if by any chance anyone should try to open it from the other side, it would still appear to be locked.

They were well pleased with their handiwork, and felt that they could afford to ignore the lightly sardonic look on Ellie's face. Instead, Richie turned to John Lamb and said, "Good God, you can't possibly marry this girl! We asked her for a Scotch half an hour ago, and she hasn't done a darn thing about it."

Nobody, not even the chauffeur who met him as he emerged from the front door of 337 Gilman Street, could have guessed what was going on in Godfrey Bellfort's mind following his meeting with Mrs. Guardi. The manservant who opened the door of his own vast house a second or two before Mr. Bellfort reached it had no idea that this rarely seen master was suffering from rage, fear, and uncertainty in equal parts. Long ago Godfrey Bellfort had realized that if you don't allow pleasure to show on your face, nobody will ever be able to recognize pain on it—if you don't show love, you will inevitably not betray hatred; pride will wear the same mask as jealousy, which will be the same mask worn by grief, or amusement, or greed.

To the manservant he said, "Bring me scrambled eggs, three eggs, dry toast and butter, hot milk and a Golden Delicious apple—in my bedroom in half an hour."

"Yes, sir."

One of the rules of all Bellfort households was that no servant should ever be seen on the inside of the door leading to the master's own suite. Bellfort passed through this door, as he always did, with a sense of exquisite relief and pleasure; he could not dismiss the memory of his niece, appalling as always, in that dark room, but he did not entirely allow her to spoil the pleasure. Indeed, somewhere at the back of his mind was the hunch that Catherine Harold Spenser, alive and living in San Francisco, posed no very great problems. He called New York, and said to the attorney who answered the phone, "Lester, find out all you can about a Mrs. Amelia Guardi of Boston, Massachusetts. Call me back any time during the night—it's urgent." He replaced the receiver, undressed tidily, and hung all his clothes up with care; then went naked into the bathroom. A little bath oil—old age tended to dry the skin—and the water not too hot; he lay in the bath with his eyes closed for ten minutes, thinking about the board meeting over which he was going to have to preside in Düsseldorf in three days' time; then he washed himself, rinsed himself with the shower, got out of the bath, and wrapped himself in a huge towel.

He had put on his pajamas, specially designed by that clever man in Rome, and his light cashmere robe, and was just brushing his fine steel-white hair when he heard the manservant come into the bedroom, following a feathery knock, and deposit the tray beside the bed. As soon as he heard the door shut again, he went into the bedroom, climbed into bed, swung the table into position, and ate his simple childish supper with simple childish pleasure. After this he read *Pride and Prejudice* for twenty minutes, took a large yellow capsule with a gulp of water, read for ten minutes more; then put the book aside, turned out the light, and was almost instantly asleep. The time was nine minutes past eight; he would sleep until five A.M. exactly. The telephone call, when it came, would barely disturb him.

• • •

Mrs. Guardi, on the other hand—as soon as Bellfort had left the house—had taken once more to that restless pacing with which, unknown to Lulu, she occupied a great deal of her time.

She thought no more about Godfrey Bellfort; what she considered to be her "victory" over him gave her no pleasure at all. In her pacing, she performed various practical tasks; she turned on the oven and put the casserole, prepared for them by the black help that morning, into it; she roused Lulu and told her that dinner would be in approximately one hour; she went to her own room and attended to her face and hair, neither of which required attention anyway. During all this her thoughts revolved around one subject, as they always did, daylong, sometimes nightlong—as they had for . . . for how long? She no longer knew how long. How long is forever—how long is obsession—how long is a second of time, or a year of time—how long is time?

She went down the passage away from the room where Lulu was fumbling about with whatever consti-tuted her evening toilette; she ignored the big circular bedroom which had been her mother's lair, went two doors past it and into a big room overlooking the garden. Fog was creeping up the hillside from the Western Addition. Mrs. Guardi did not look at it; she locked the door and stood leaning against it with her eyes closed.

This had been his room. On that very bed, one afternoon when her mother had been at the beauty salon, he had taken her for the first time, broken her virginity and made her his—forever. She crossed to the bed and lay down on it, face down as if, even now, she could catch something of the smell of his adored, his magnificent body. Dear God, what love they had made on this bed! "Again," she would cry, "again!" And again he would possess her . . . again . . . again . . .

How old had she been? Just seventeen—and she had desired him from the moment he had entered the house, entered her life, laughing, holding her stupid mother by the arm and laughing.

Mrs. Guardi rolled over onto her back and stared at the ceiling. If only she could weep, but that was denied her. God had denied her tears—it was part of her punishment. Had He . . . could it conceivably be possible that He had denied her reunion as well? Was God that cruel? Was Eternal Justice that inflexible? The yearning, the seemingly endless search, the finding of Lulu, the agony of patience which she (so impatient a woman) had endured—was it possible that all these things counted as nothing in the sight of God, who was a Jealous God—beautiful and jealous as Michael had been beautiful and jealous (but that was blasphemy)?

She moaned a little, rolling her head this way and that on the bare mattress, as she had done night after night since coming back to this house. "Michael?" She whispered it very quietly but with agonized intensity. "Mikey, oh Mikey, my darling, I know you're there. Come to me. Come to me tonight. Speak to me—just once. Tell me you still love me—tell me you . . . you . . . you forgive me."

The head rolled more urgently this way and that in a kind of paroxysm. If only she could cry—if only there could be tears, blessed healing tears! It was her punishment.

"Michael, I beg you, I *beg you*, come to me tonight,

speak to me through her. All the others have spoken, why not you? Oh God, let him speak to me tonight!"

She had lied—was that why he didn't come? She had lied to Lulu, who was herself the door through which he could, he *must*, reach her. But if she hadn't lied, telling that absurd story about writing a book, acting out the hours of "research" during which, in reality, she had been sitting in the St. Francis Hotel or watching but not seeing some trivial movie—if she hadn't pretended to find the house with the aid of a detective agency, if she hadn't led Lulu on with ridiculous dreams of fame and glory, Lulu would never have uprooted herself from that dim, malodorous room in London, would never have crossed half the world.

The end had to justify the means, surely even a Jealous God could see that—*particularly* a jealous God? She wished no harm on Lulu, she wished no harm on the girl who lived in the studio, God knew that.

"Then send him to me tonight. Let him speak to me through her mouth. Let him love me and forgive me in Thy name. I pray, I pray, I pray. Michael, come to me! Blessed Archangel Michael with thy sword, whose body hath possessed mine, yea, on this very bed, whose sword hath pierced my body and made me thine . . ."

Lulu had reasoned with herself; she could hardly believe it; the result (as it often is—even with those more adept at reasoning than Lulu) was what she had wanted all along: to continue the "work" with Mrs. Guardi, and to produce a book which would confound all Doubting Thomases, not to mention Jackie Jenkins, making Lulu famous, rich, and venerated in the process. She still had misgivings—indeed, she bored Mrs.

Guardi all through dinner with her misgivings—but in her own mind she had done her duty; she had warned Ellie; her conscience was at peace—or rather, it ought to have been at peace, she really didn't know why it wasn't.

Mrs. Guardi, even more calm and reasonable than was her wont tonight, sat through the misgivings with a patience which made Job seem small. Like her uncle, Godfrey Bellfort, and for reasons not so very different, she had hidden her true feelings for so long, from so many people, including a husband and two adopted children, that she could barely show them if she tried. As far as she was concerned now, only one thing mattered: the camel, in spite of protestations, was not going to balk at the hill. ("Dear God, let him speak to me—let him speak to me, *just once*, tonight!")

John Lamb came quietly back through the door and bolted it again behind him. Ellie and her brother were sitting at the table with their wine. Lamb said, "They're still in the dining room; I can't hear what they're saying—there's nowhere to hide in that hall."

The curtains were closed, the candle had been lighted and placed on the table; the tape recorder, that ridiculous stage property, made ready. (Mrs. Guardi didn't even know how to work it properly, but it had betrayed her.) All that was missing was the Fabergé Easter egg. Lulu looked around for it—not that the egg in itself mattered, but she needed something.

Amelia Guardi came back to the table from the shadows of the room carrying a small book. She said, not for the first time, "Tonight, Lulu, I feel that we

must somehow contact this man, Michael Burke; he's
the key, I'm sure of it."

"Key?"

Mrs. Guardi sighed inwardly. "It all pivots on him—
the things that happened here long ago. Before we can
start the actual writing of our book, we must speak to
him, surely you see that?"

"Our book!" Lulu slipped into a delicious reverie—
our book.

Mrs. Guardi allowed the reverie to continue for a
good half-minute before repeating, "We must speak to
him; he knows the secret we're looking for."

Mrs. Jenkins nodded dreamily. She could feel him not
far away—the dark ominous presence which alarmed
her so much. It was true that all the others had spoken
except him; perhaps this was her fault—perhaps the
aversion she felt for him acted as some sort of barrier;
she must banish it.

As if sensing this thought, Amelia Guardi held out
the small leatherbound volume. "I found this on the
shelf; it seems that it was his—his own personal
property, Lulu; not like the Easter egg which he bought
for her, for Stella."

Lulu took the book. As soon as the sausage-fingers
closed around it a tremor shook her whole body; she
looked at the book with grave suspicion. *Great Love
Poems of the Ages.* She snorted but made no comment.
What did he know about love, that animal, forever
grunting and rutting with this body or that? She opened
the book; on the flyleaf was written: "M from C. Every
word is from me to you." Michael from . . . C? There
was a C, wasn't there? Ah yes, hovering always at the

corner of things, never seen. Catherine. She said it aloud: "Catherine?"

"I suppose so, yes." Mrs. Guardi turned away from the pale-green eyes which were so blind and yet saw so much. Loving Catherine, seventeen years old—foolish Catherine—lost Catherine—idiot Catherine!

She looked back at the fat woman with the book in her hand, and thought that she recognized the expression that suffused the flaccid face. "Does it . . . ?" No, keep the excitement, the anguish out of the voice. "Does it seem to bring him any closer?"

Lulu nodded. "He's here."

Mrs. Guardi's heart leapt inside her like an imprisoned bird; she could hardly hear through the panic beating of its wings.

"But she . . . Catherine . . ." Lulu frowned.

"What about her?" A foolish question perhaps—a vain and foolish question; she regretted it.

"I never . . . never see her. She's never here." Lulu opened her eyes wide and stared at Amelia Guardi, who immediately thought, Oh my God, she knows, she's guessed.

Quickly she said, "Think of him, Lulu; think of Michael; we must speak to Michael."

Lulu looked away. She had been about to say something—something important. Never mind, she had lost it now; and he was very close; he filled the room, clumsily and brutally, as he had done so many times before. Always she had resisted him, but tonight . . . Our book! No, tonight she must not resist him. She must follow him down that passage, through the door covered in red baize, towards the studio where the woman waited for him. There was always a woman waiting for him . . .

It had been Richie's turn to make the reconnaissance. He came back looking pleased with himself. "They're in the small library."

Excitement jumped inside John Lamb. "Have they locked the door?"

"No. You can see through the keyhole. There's a candle on the table—the one you saw, I guess; and the tape recorder."

Ellie's amusement had forsaken her, replaced by an emotion she could not quite define. She, too, was excited, but in a way that she remembered from her childhood, a kind of reluctant fear uppermost. (Why climb the wall? There might be bears on the other side—or snakes—or even an old man with one leg. As a child, cripples had always terrified her.)

"What are they doing?"

"Looking at some book. Come on!"

The plan was for Richie and Lamb to investigate, by the keyhole and if possible a window. Ellie would stand by the intercommunicating door, ready to close and bolt it behind them if they decided to beat a hasty and hopefully unseen retreat. She watched the two of them, both wearing sneakers, disappear down the cold dark passage. As they turned the corner Lamb switched on a flashlight. Ellie was torn between a desire to giggle and to call them sharply back; certainly she had no desire to accompany them.

The baize-covered door squeaked slightly as they opened it; they paused, like mice discovered on the bread bin, holding their breaths. The whole of the big house was blanketed in a thick dull silence.

After perhaps thirty seconds they allowed the door to close, protesting slightly, on the weight of the spring that held it shut. There was now no need for the flashlight; the passage was lit by a radiance from the hall around the next corner. A line of light shone under the door which was their target. As they approached it, they heard the sound of deep, perhaps agonized, perhaps even bestial breathing. It rooted them both; sent a prickle of fear up both their spines . . .

Mrs. Guardi watched as the wide-open green eyes rolled slowly upwards and disappeared from sight. The still flame of the candle was now reflected in the blank, slightly veined whites. It was horrifying but it no longer made her shudder. The stertorous breathing became lighter—lighter yet—faded into the long, steady, widely spaced breaths of deep trance. The hand that held the book of poetry (*M from C. Every word is from me to you*) trembled slightly and was still again.

Amelia Guardi leaned forward eagerly, matt black eyes fixed on the extraordinary face across the table. Dear God, let him speak. Michael, darling Mikey, speak to me! It was a silent scream—a silent scream that she had uttered every single night that they had sat here like this. She could contain it no longer; her voice low and shaking, she said, "Michael? Michael Burke, are you there?"

To her fury, she was answered by the voice of her mother: "It's not true, you're lying, you always lie. No, don't go on—I won't listen, I refuse to listen. Stop, stop, *stop!*"

Mrs. Guardi gasped, "Oh dear God, not you!"

Whining, full of fear and self-pity, Stella went on: "What are you trying to do to me? You know I'm not well, you know the doctor said I wasn't to get upset . . ."

In a voice full of anguish her daughter cried, "*Mikey, where are you?*"

Outside the door, Richie straightened up from the keyhole; in the dim light he looked pale and scared. Lamb knelt quickly—just in time to see Amelia Guardi's face as she leaned across the table; he was shocked to notice how pale and strained, even old, it looked.

The voice of Stella Harold Spenser dwindled away and Lulu's head dropped onto her chest, almost touching the book which she was clasping against it. Mrs. Guardi leaned back, so that he could no longer see her; she had fought for self-control and won, because, when she spoke again, it was with a return to her old tone, tense and quiet: "Michael, are you there? We must speak to Michael Burke."

Lulu made no movement, continuing to breathe deeply and slowly.

Amelia Guardi watched her, panic mounting inside her. She knew he was there; Lulu herself had said that he was there; why didn't he answer? The thought that he might never, never in a thousand and one nights, answer choked her with panic. She leaned forward again. "Mikey, please speak to me, my darling—I know you're there. Mikey, it's Catherine, it's Cathie—speak to me."

Lamb straightened up from the keyhole and his eyes met Richie's. Catherine! Had one of them spoken, or was it simply that the enormity of what they had just heard leapt between them like a short circuit?

Suddenly from behind the door came the sound of a man's laughter. Lamb gasped. Richie bent swiftly to look. He saw that Lulu had raised those terrible sightless eyes and was once more staring at the candle. The laughter which emerged from her mouth did not shake her obese body, and this made it all the more terrifying. But not as terrifying as the glimpse of Mrs. Guardi's face which he caught as she leapt to her feet, leaning across the table; for on it was a look of girlish pleasure, almost of ecstasy.

"Oh Mikey . . ." Her voice wavered on the edge of tears. "Oh my darling, speak to me."

If the laughter was incredible, the voice was even more so; it was a man's voice, a young man's voice, yet the vocal cords of a fat old woman were producing it. What it said was incredible too; it said, "Oh Catherine, for Christ's sake, fuck off!"

Mrs. Guardi let out a cry, one hand pressed to her mouth. The laughter burst out again—the laughter of Michael Burke, not a pleasant sound to hear.

Amelia Guardi swayed across the table; for a moment it seemed that in her agony she was about to strike Lulu Jenkins. She controlled herself, her face working with emotion; her voice pleading fiercely, she said, "No, Mikey, please—not that. Remember the good times, *please* remember the good times. Tell me you loved me. Tell me . . . Mikey, for the love of God, tell me you . . . you forgive me."

Evidently there was no love of God in Michael Burke. The cruel voice that issued from Lulu's mouth said, "Oh for Christ's sake. So we had a good time, you're a great lay, so what—it's over, it was over long ago, you shouldn't have gone back to school . . . Oh for Christ's sake, Catherine, if there's one thing I can't stand, it's a sniveling woman, get out of my way!"

"Mikey? Mikey, come back. Don't go—I know where you're going." There was silence. Mrs. Guardi gasped through tears, "Mikey, don't go away, don't leave me." Silence. It was almost as though Lulu had stopped breathing; better for Amelia Guardi if she had, for what happened next was worse than what had gone before. Lulu's mouth—mouth of a recording angel or mouth of the netherworld—opened to release a ripple of girlish giggling. Agonized, Mrs. Guardi banged the table with both fists, making the candle jump. She cried out, *"No!"* in a strong and terrible voice, but there was no stopping now the self-inflicted torture which it had cost her so much time and so much money to start.

The giggling formed itself into words: "Ooh, you are awful! Ooh, Mikey, no—not here. Mikey, not here, someone might see . . ."

Mrs. Guardi's head had fallen forward; her eyes were screwed tight shut; a low animal moan of pain escaped from her.

"Ooh Mikey, mind my *dress!*" A gasp of pleasure or pain and labored breathing. It had seemed to be the girl's breathing, but now became recognizable as that of a man.

Again, uselessly, Mrs. Guardi gasped, *"No!"*

The breathing molded itself into the voice of Michael Burke, slurred by lust, whispering, "Go to the studio, you know the studio? Go there and wait for me, I won't be a minute . . . Yes, I want you too, baby—feel that—go on, feel that!"

Amelia Guardi's agony suddenly found voice in a terrible cry of rage and anguish, of lost hopes and unbearable truth. At the same moment she swore (she would always swear) that she saw the shape, the shadow of a man, run past the table behind Lulu. Certainly the candle flame fluttered wildly and the room seemed to be full of movement, full of a crackling energy which, a second later, seemed to explode. The heavy candlestick left the table as if swept by a strong and resentful hand; it smacked straight into the face of Lulu Jenkins, who let out a strangled gasp. Mrs. Guardi screamed again. Lulu sagged forward onto the table.

Outside the door, John Lamb and Richie seemed to be thrown back against the wall by a violent force which (they both said later) was almost visible. This force was so strong that Richie's head hit the carved doorpost and immediately began to bleed. John Lamb recovered just in time to hear the squeak of the baize-covered door and the impact as it was thrown back against the wall. An instant later he heard what was unmistakably Ellie's voice raised in a wail of what he took to be terror.

As he turned to run he was aware that the door to the study had been thrown open by Mrs. Guardi; she looked totally demented and seemed to see neither of them. She shouted, "No, for God's sake, no!" But by that time he was running. His mind barely recorded the fact that the baize-covered door was not swinging, which it certainly would have been if somebody had actually passed through it violently a few seconds before. He swung around the corner of the passage and saw in front of him the open doorway leading through the "closet" and into Ellie's bedroom. As he leapt towards it, he heard Ellie cry out again.

He flung himself through the door and came face to face with her—or at least with somebody or something wearing her hair and clothes. Before he could lose momentum she whipped out the carving knife from behind her back and stabbed at him savagely; he fell back, trying to evade her. The thing that was or was not Ellie came after him, knife raised, stabbing and stabbing—eyes wide and seemingly sightless, mouth wide, saliva dribbling; came after him, stabbing, stabbing. With horror, he saw his own blood spattering the wall . . .

Two

THE SMALL living room of the studio seemed crowded. Godfrey Bellfort sat enthroned in the only comfortable chair, but managed to make it seem hard and upright. Mrs. Guardi sat at the table, staring at her clasped hands which rested on it, never raising her odd black eyes. Richie sat on the sofa next to John Lamb, who lay back on a pile of pillows, looking pale and haggard. Robert Hillier leaned against the wall between Lamb and the bedroom door; in this way he could keep an eye on both his patients, for Ellie was in her bed, deep in drugged sleep. Lulu Jenkins was not present; she lay dead where she had fallen, in the study of the big house. It was now three A.M.

Richie had wasted no time in calling Dr. Hillier, who had found a house full of people in need of medical attention. He immediately appreciated that there was nothing he could do for poor Lulu—that Mrs. Guardi was a case for later, and possibly extensive, treatment, and that the contusion on Richie's head was not serious. Ellie lay unconscious on the bedroom floor, the knife still in her hand; Hillier gave her a shot and, with her brother's help, put her to bed. As for Lamb, the wounds were not as disastrous as they had first seemed, but he had lost a lot of blood and was in a state of shock. On the whole, Hillier's most difficult job had been to persuade Richie that there was now only one possible course open to them: they must call Godfrey Bellfort. During all this, Mrs. Guardi had sat as patiently and silently as she sat now; she seemed totally detached; not even the sprawling mass of Lulu's body seemed to disturb her; when spoken to, she said nothing.

Richie had finally given in to Hillier's arguments only when the doctor told him that he knew, from his father-in-law's private papers, that this would not be the first crisis that Bellfort had been forced to supervise at 337 Gilman Street. (In this respect Robert Hillier had been reading between the lines; he did not yet know how true, shatteringly true, his guess would turn out to be.) Bellfort, who had not yet gone back to sleep following his expected call from an attorney in New York, surprised the doctor by his spry response to the emergency. He had dressed quickly but with care, and now, upright in the only comfortable chair, looked like any elderly gentleman summoned at, say, nine o'clock in the evening from a dinner party, a white silk scarf neatly tucked into his black coat. When he finally spoke, his voice was as dry and precise as it would be in two days' time when he came to preside over that board meeting in Düsseldorf.

He said, "If I don't tell you the truth, you"—the granite eyes flickered over the doctor and the two young men—"are going to start asking questions—of yourselves, of each other, even of outsiders. This is not desirable. As I've said before, Dr. Hillier will keep what I'm about to say to himself because he is under oath, to his profession and to his . . . private conscience.

"You"—the eyes passed over Lamb and rested on Richie's for a second—"will keep quiet because you both love that girl in there; indiscretion on your part could land her with a charge of attempted murder; other unfortunate details would then be unearthed. I hope I make myself clear?"

It was obvious that he did. The cold grey eyes grew yet colder as they swiveled to the woman who sat so unutterably still, gazing at her hands. "As for you, Catherine . . ." He did not try to keep an edge of satisfaction out of his voice; the scene in the darkening room still rankled too sharply. "For the second time you have been an accessory to violent death. I think the law might find 'accessory' too mild a word. Your mental state might also be questioned; information reached me from Boston not long ago that you have three times been admitted to a certain private nursing home there; I don't imagine it is so private that the doctors could not be persuaded to make a written statement."

Mrs. Guardi said nothing; the knuckles of her clasped hands grew a little whiter, that was all.

"I shall make no effort to draw parallels or medical conclusions, that is not my province; but obviously the . . . psychic dabbling of two stupid women has in some way caused the past and the present to become confused. Only a fool would deny that, and in my opinion, only a fool would inquire into it any further."

He paused for a moment; then sighed lightly—at the folly of mankind presumably; then leaned back a little and looked up at the ceiling. "On April the fifth, 1938, my sister, Stella Harold Spenser, killed her second husband, Michael Burke, here in this studio. She was not . . . not in her right mind, and had not been so for some time.

"Her motive was jealousy—insane jealousy. He had never been faithful to her from the day of their marriage; he was an unspeakable young man and richly deserved to die."

Mrs. Guardi's clenched hands parted . . . and re-arranged themselves. The dry voice continued: "He had conducted squalid affairs with numberless females, including his own stepdaughter. Who seduced whom in that case is open to doubt." He looked at his niece with merciless eyes, but she remained absolutely still, a figure of stone.

"You probably wonder why, if he had been unfaithful to his wife for so long, she was driven to do what she did at the particular time that she did it. She was driven to it by her own daughter, who had, naturally, by that young man's standards, lost her place in his bed to the next in line. She was beside herself with fury and grief."

Mrs. Guardi drew in a deep breath and closed her eyes.

"To give Catherine her due, I must say that she was deeply in love with Michael Burke—besotted by him; she was seventeen—a cruel age; she had never been . . . noted for her self-control.

"However, there is no possible excuse for what she did: working and working on the already diseased mind of her mother until in the end she pushed it into the abyss. Of course, the final straw for poor Stella was when her own daughter revealed that she herself had been Burke's mistress—that he had carried on a lengthy affair with her directly under his wife's nose, and often, when she was away from home, in her own bed. I'm sure he found the experience most titillating. As I say, he was unspeakable.

"He often made assignations here in this studio; Catherine knew of one of them; she told her mother. When he opened the door she was waiting for him with a knife."

He was silent again for what seemed a long time; again he sighed. "I myself am not without guilt. I loved my sister very much; I had no intention of seeing her dragged through the muck of a murder trial. I used . . . *mis*used, if you will, my money and my power to cover the whole thing up. It wasn't difficult. The servants had heard nothing; their mistress was often ill in bed for days; Burke was often away for days . . ." He closed his eyes and shook his head. "I have no intention of going into details. Catherine was by now terrified by what she had done—of what the consequences might be. Luckily, her brother was away from home. I sent her to my ranch, and I . . . arranged that Mr. and Mrs. Michael Burke should leave for Europe. I myself took my sister to the establishment on Lake Geneva where she lived out the rest of her wretched life. Various paragraphs appeared in the press; newspapermen can always be bought. I suppose it was taken for granted that after a while my sister had grown tired of her revolting young husband, and that he returned to . . . whatever cesspool had generated him." He fell silent; then nodded to himself as if satisfied that what he had said was all that he wished to say. "That is all. God alone knows, I thought it was enough. But now . . ."

His bleak eyes traveled around the room, taking in

the weary faces, the girl lying drugged on the bed, the bloodstains that spattered the wall. "Well, this is a simpler matter. Luckily, I have good friends in this town. The police must be called at once; you"—to Mrs. Guardi—"will say only what I instruct you to say. I shall make it possible for you to leave for the East in the morning. Disobey me in any way and I assure you that I shall have you committed.

"You, Hillier, will look after that girl and the young Englishman. Send your account to me." (Would he, Hillier was wondering, have his father-in-law's strength of mind, and thus benefit some children's hospital? He had been wanting a bigger yacht for some years.)

"You," said Godfrey Bellfort to Richie, "will buy some paint and see to those walls yourself—the carpet, too, if necessary." The hard grey eyes moved over them all for the last time. "You are all reasonably intelligent people. I'm sure I don't have to repeat the warnings with which I began this . . . distasteful peroration."

Presumably he took the silence which followed this remark as a sign of understanding and compliance, which indeed it was. He nodded more briskly. "Now—here is exactly what each of you will do and say . . ."

Three

THE BIG house stands empty.

Shortly after her return to Boston, Mrs. Amelia Guardi suffered "a mild heart attack" and retired to a sanatorium. She planned to leave after a couple of weeks, but that was nearly five months ago, and she is still there. She plans to leave shortly.

Godfrey Bellfort was also in Boston for a few hours prior to his trip to Germany. He is now resting at one of his houses, some say in Yucatán; others say that he has no house in Yucatán and is in Turkey; nobody knows for sure; nobody ever has and in all likelihood nobody ever will.

The police dealt swiftly and politely with the death of Mrs. Louise Jenkins; their doctor agreed with Hillier that she carried far too much weight and that her heart just couldn't take the strain.

Ellie Owen Spenser, after spending a week at her brother's apartment, left with him on a long and unhurried vacation, starting in Japan.

John Lamb was in a nursing home for several weeks, all expenses paid by Mr. Godfrey Bellfort, naturally. It was a very discreet nursing home not far from San Luis Obispo; he then went back to Europe, via Dallas as planned. He wonders whether, in her journeying with her brother, Ellie will pass through Paris, the city in which they first met, where they were so happy. He hopes so, because he is still in love with her and still wants to marry her.

Dr. Robert Hillier has just bought a new yacht, much larger and more impressive than his old one.

And the big house stands empty. In that emptiness there are sometimes strange flurries of movement. Draft probably, all old houses are drafty. Sometimes in foggy nights a passer-by has imagined that he heard voices raised in argument, but fog often plays odd tricks with sound; the voices probably come from some other house lower down the steep slopes of Pacific Heights.

Like many another big empty house, Number 337 Gilman Street is even said to be haunted; an old lady maintains that she saw a fat, shapeless woman staring down at the street from an upstairs window; but the old lady's eyesight has been failing for years, and anyway—as anyone who matters knows—337 Gilman Street used to belong to the Harold Spensers, and no member of that beautiful, wealthy, and charming San Franciscan family was ever known to be fat or shapeless.

About the Author

Philip Loraine was born in Casablanca, the illegitimate son of an Italian Contessa and a stoker in the Danish Navy. He was educated at Eton and Wormwood Scrubs, and by the age of five he and his mother were smuggling diamonds into the United States inside his favorite teddy bear . . .

What a pity that mystery writers are never such interesting creatures! Philip Loraine is in fact a pseudonym. Under his real name he has written a number of other novels and film scripts, working both in Europe and the U.S.A. Among other jobs he has been a sailor in the navy, a journalist in Fleet Street and a dishwasher in Paris. Although he is British by nationality he does not live in Britain, spending most of his time either in France or in California, trying to make up his mind where he really wants to settle down. He has visited and sometimes lived in some two dozen countries, so it is obvious that one of his likes is traveling; he is also very fond of writing, the sun, good food, painting (when he has time) and music. His dislikes include politicians and the current sickness of selfishness and violence. He thinks the world is a remarkable and beautiful place but is not so sure about the two-legged mammal that dominates it.